A huge mass of fear clogged Annora's throat.

"We have approached Percival Thornby and his mother with what we feel is a solution to a number of problems. Ours and theirs," the Reverend Baxter announced.

"Please," Annora begged, looking from the man to his wife, then back again. "Please, don't tell me I—"

"Oh, do not resort to useless entreaties," his wife piped in. "It has been obvious to us from the very first that you have been anything but grateful we took you into our home."

"But that's not true—"

Mrs. Baxter raised a hand to silence her. "Regardless of your denials, I fear your actions have spoken far more blatantly than anything you might try to say now. Let me assure you that for some time I have been on the verge of complete and utter despair over your spiteful deeds. For such an opportunity to arise now in order to benefit the lot of us, it can only have come from the Almighty's own hand."

"You do happen to be of marriageable age," the reverend explained before Annora could respond. "And for us, your legal guardians, to be able to arrange such an advantageous match for you is an answer to prayer. We can rest in knowing you will be comfortably taken care of. The Thornby wealth is considerable. If our Mirah wasn't so young, we would not hesitate a bit in securing such a splendid match for her."

"But. . .but I. . .can't—"

SALLY LAITY, having successfully written several novels, including a co-authored series for Tyndale, three Barbour novellas, and five Heartsongs, this author's favorite thing these days is counseling new authors via the Internet. Sally always loved to write, and after her four children were grown she took college writing courses and attended Christian writing conferences. She has written both historical and contemporary romances, and considers it a joy to know that the Lord can touch other hearts through her stories. She makes her home in Bakersfield, California, with her husband and enjoys being a grandma.

Books by Sally Laity

HEARTSONG PRESENTS
HP4—Reflections of the Heart
HP31—Dream Spinner
HP81—Better Than Friends
HP236—Valiant Heart

If the Prospect Pleases

Sally Laity

Heartsong Presents

To Randie, my sweet daughter-in-law. I'm so glad the Lord brought you into our lives.

Many thanks to Andrea Boeshaar, Gloria Brandt, and Dianna Crawford, for their patient shredding and tireless encouragement. May God bless all your writing efforts.

A note from the author:
I love to hear from my readers! You may correspond with me by writing: **Sally Laity**
Author Relations
PO Box 719
Uhrichsville, OH 44683

ISBN 1-57748-486-X

IF THE PROSPECT PLEASES

All Scripture quotations are from the Authorized King James Version of the Bible unless otherwise noted.

Cover design by Jodi Reed.

PRINTED IN THE U.S.A.

prologue

Philadelphia 1875

Nothing would ever be the same. Ever. Annora Nolan yearned with all her heart to awaken from the nightmare. . . but the smell of the moist ground in the fenced area behind the church more than proved it was all very real.

Last week it had been Papa, her copper-haired hero, who had succumbed to the dreaded typhoid. Now folks had gathered to lay away her soft-spoken mama as well. Clutching her damp woolen cloak closer against the chill, Annora scarcely heard the minister's voice droning through the funeral scriptures. She was too busy praying she would die, too. . .though in her heart she doubted the plea would be granted.

Adding to her misery, the relentless October drizzle falling from the leaden sky had fused the brilliant hues of autumn into sodden clumps of burgundy, gold, and brown, heavy masses never to be separated again. To Annora, the pathetic sight seemed a symbol of her own future, and the thought sent a desolate shiver through her as the wind plastered her wet skirt to her legs.

Gazing at the closed coffin through a blur of tears, Annora lowered her eyelids against the ache in her heart. What would become of her now?

"Come along, child."

The service must have ended. Realizing that someone had addressed her, Annora turned and looked up into the face of the Reverend Baxter's wife, Millicent. The hazel eyes in the woman's plump but refined features expressed abundant sympathy. "You'll be coming home with us for the night," she explained gently, extending a gloved hand.

"But. . .my things. I–I need—"

"I'll send our housekeeper for them presently. It's all right. Come along now."

Annora swept an uneasy glance from the black-clad figure to the woman's other side, where the couple's daughter, Mirah, stared with brown-eyed coolness at Annora from beneath the brim of her velvet and satin bonnet. An exquisitely beautiful girl two years younger than Annora, not a muscle in her perfect oval face moved, even when a sharp gust splayed a brunette ringlet across her cheek. Annora had never been fond of the overly pampered girl, but she knew she had no other recourse. After all, it was just for one night.

❧

Alone in Mirah's second-story bedroom while the younger girl visited the privy outside before turning in, Annora could hear the Reverend Baxter's words drifting up from the room directly below. She shifted uncomfortably on the pallet that had been laid out for her on the floor.

"Fourteen is rather old to be relegated to the Children's Home, Millicent, my dear."

"I'm fully aware of that, Phineas," his wife replied, normally the dominant voice of the household. "But I fail to see what else is to be done—short of trying to place her ourselves where she might be useful."

"We could assume guardianship," the reverend went on in his familiar nasal tone. "We've known her since she was a young girl, and there's hardly a more mannerly or more respectful young person in our entire flock. Besides, she has no other living relatives, and her parents numbered among the founding families of this church. It would deem us well not to overlook their support of our parish over the years."

"Quite. However—"

"The matter needn't be decided this very instant," he interrupted, and Annora could envision any number of typical gestures he might have used to cut in. His slight frame a mere shadow in comparison to his wife's more fleshy presence, he sounded uncharacteristically firm in his resolve. "Do not forget the influential families among our congregation who look favorably upon such acts of benevolence—who might even consider it our Christian duty to take in the girl as our ward. And it very well may be."

After a brief lapse, he started in again. "I shudder to imagine how tongues would wag should we turn their daughter out in her hour of need."

Annora held her breath in the ensuing pregnant silence while her fate was being decided downstairs.

"Bear in mind," the pastor continued, "the girl would be a help to Nellie, to say nothing of being company for our dear Mirah. We've always wished God had blessed us with another child. Perhaps this is His way of granting that wish."

"I hadn't thought of that." A note of optimism rang in his wife's tone. "The idea might have merit after all."

"What idea?" Mirah asked sweetly, obviously having come back inside.

"Mirah, dear, your father and I were relating how wonderful it might be for you if we were to have another young girl living with us. Someone near your own age to keep you company."

"Oh."

The tightly contained emotion in the answer made Annora cringe, and tears stung her eyes. It was no secret among the young people at church that Mirah Baxter reveled in her lofty position as only child, daughter of the pastor. Her gifts went beyond mere exotic beauty to exceptional musical talent as well. And when Annora had been chosen over her as soloist in the last two recitals, she had pouted for days. . .but never in the presence of her parents, before whom she maintained guileless behavior at all times.

No, Mirah would not welcome having to share her life of

privilege, especially with a foundling who happened to be a little older than herself and who might be given extra privileges for that reason. Annora drew the quilts more snugly around her, trying to squelch feelings of mortification threatening to overwhelm even her unspeakable grief.

"We've not as yet undertaken permanent arrangements," the minister explained. "We're merely considering possibilities."

"Then permit me to voice my feelings, Father," Mirah pleaded. "I far prefer things as they have always been—you, Mother, and me. Pray, let's keep it that way. Please?"

"I'll give your wishes proper consideration, Daughter," the Reverend Baxter replied. "But I must weigh this matter very carefully. And be assured that my decision will be final. Now, be a good girl and go to bed. Tomorrow is another day."

"Yes, of course, Father," she returned, all sweetness again. "Good night. Good night, Mother."

"Good night, angel."

As the younger girl's slippers padded up the open staircase, Annora turned her face to the wall and feigned sleep. She was careful not to move even the slightest bit as the door swung closed—though she could almost feel Mirah's dark eyes stabbing her like ice picks. When the rustle of embroidered silk indicated the daughter of the household had removed her wrap and slipped into the warmth of her canopied feather bed, Annora slowly released a pent-up breath. But not until Mirah's disgruntled huffs settled into the even rhythm of sleep did Annora give in to her sorrow.

❧

To her amazement, Annora found life with the Baxters quite bearable. The minister and his wife went out of their way to make her feel welcome and a part of the family, which helped immensely to get her through the initial crushing sadness over the loss of her parents. And—even more surprising—Mirah, too, seemed to accept her.

Or so she thought.

But when an heirloom timepiece unaccountably disappeared from Mrs. Baxter's jewelry chest, only to turn up in the drawer designated for Annora's belongings, things took a decided turn. Annora, her cheeks aflame as she stammered her denial of guilt, would remember until her dying day the shock and disappointment on her guardians' faces. . .and the unabashed innocence on Mirah's. That was when Annora sensed that despite all the Baxters' well-meaning gestures toward her, she would forever remain an outsider in this home.

And that was just the beginning.

A spattering of other rather minor infractions pointing to Annora occurred over the next few months. But not until Mirah's handmade quilt met its ruin did things finally come to a head.

"I truly regret that my husband and I found it necessary to take this step, Annora," Mrs. Baxter said, standing in the doorway of the chilly attic room. She had the grace to look ill at ease as she flicked a glance around the stark quarters. "But since it appears the fate of your very soul is in question, you leave us no choice but to take drastic measures. One must learn there are consequences for one's actions.

"Hereafter, except for those periods when you are performing your duties, you will remain here by yourself until such time as we feel you are once again deserving of our trust. I suggest you use the solitude to reflect on what lies ahead of you if you do not mend your ways."

"Yes, ma'am." Annora gave a dutiful nod as the minister's wife departed without further word, the sound of her button-top shoes fading to silence as she returned downstairs.

Gloating in this, her most recent victory, Mirah leaned against the doorjamb and crossed her arms. "This should do quite nicely. . .for you."

Refusing to acknowledge the satisfied smirk on the younger girl's face, Annora breezed past her with an airy smile and came the rest of the way into the tiny room graced only by the

hazy light from a small dormer window. She set the belongings she'd carried up the stairs onto the narrow bedstead abutting the jointure of low wall and sloped ceiling. "Yes. It's quite
an improvement, actually. I rather like it." Hands on her hips,
she hiked her chin and looked about as if admiring the most
splendid of accommodations in all of Philadelphia.

Mirah's jaw gaped. "Indeed. Well, now that I've managed
to oust you from my room, I'll concentrate on the next step—
getting you out of this house. It should be a simple enough
feat, I'm sure." A vicious sneer moved across her proud lips.

Unable to come up with a suitable retort, Annora presented
her back.

The Baxter's stout housekeeper, Nellie Henderson, trudged
in from the landing just then, her arms filled with bedding. She
dumped the burden on the cot. "La, such a climb," she panted,
placing one hand over her cushiony bosom, which rose and
fell in time with her labored breathing. Her fair cheeks
remained a bright rosy pink beneath her faded blond coronet
until the short gasps lengthened to more normal intervals.

"Sorry you've gone to so much trouble," Annora said with
true concern, ignoring Mirah's blatant look of contempt as the
younger girl turned on her heel and traipsed back downstairs.

Mrs. Henderson glanced after her, then met Annora's gaze
with a shake of her frazzled head. "This is a fair disgrace,
miss, that's what it is," she said in a near whisper. "Puttin' a
young thing like you way up here by yourself, with us still in
the throes of winter. You'll not have a lick of heat, except
what might waft up from below. Don't know what madam is
thinkin'. She and the reverend have always been such soft-
hearted folks, up till now."

"Oh, well, no matter how cold the attic gets, it'll be nothing compared to what I had to endure sharing their only
daughter's room," Annora muttered. Then she flushed with
embarrassment. "Forgive me. That must sound ungrateful. It
was more than unselfish of the reverend and his wife to

become my guardians. They've been nothing but generous and loving to me."

"Yes, well, nobody except the two of us knows who really rules this household," the older woman continued with an understanding nod. "Let me tell you, things changed around here once that little dickens made her appearance in the world. And not for the better, I don't mind sayin'. The way her parents dote on her. . .*tsk tsk.* Of course, she acts the perfect angel around them. But to think they actually believed you would deliberately pour a bottle of ink over the counterpane her grandmother finished mere weeks before she died!"

Slowly wagging her head, the woman bent over and began unfolding the topmost quilt on the pile she'd brought upstairs.

"Please, you needn't do this," Annora said, gathering the heavy folds the housekeeper was in the process of shaking out. "I'll make my own bed, then I'll come and help with dinner."

"Well," came the hesitant response, "if you're sure. I must say, it's been a blessing havin' an extra pair of hands since you arrived, what with lookin' after the parsonage *and* the church by myself since old Mr. Baldwin crossed over."

Annora smiled. "I don't mind daily chores. I'd rather keep busy than sit around reading dime novels and eating bonbons."

"Like Her Highness, you mean. Well, one of these days the little miss is sure to get her comeuppance. See if she don't. The Lord will see to that in His time." With a conspiratorial wink, the housekeeper nodded and moved toward the doorway but paused briefly before departing. "Now that you've got a room to yourself," she began, grimacing as her glance swept the dismal quarters, "there's somethin' you should know. I managed to rescue a few of your mama's special things for you. . .kept them out of the auction that was held to pay your father's creditors."

"You didn't!" Filled with the first real comfort she'd felt since her parents had passed away, Annora flew to give her a hug.

"Now, now," the amiable woman murmured, patt

Annora's back before easing away. "I couldn't see how a few baubles would make a lick of difference one way or the other. Anyways, a gal should have somethin' to remind her of her family. I was waitin' for a time when Miss Uppity wouldn't be stickin' her royal nose into your business. We can tote them up after while, when you and me fetch the rest of your clothes and things."

"Thank you. Oh, thank you, Mrs. Henderson."

" 'Twas the least I could do, miss. Only right you should have them. Oh, and I'm sure I can rummage up some extra curtains and a rug to help brighten this place up a little. We'll get it set to rights soon enough."

As the housekeeper took her leave, Annora couldn't hold back a smile at the joyous thought of having some of Mama's precious possessions to hold in her hands again, but it quickly wilted as she settled back and took a closer look at her bleak surroundings. Bare and harsh in its grim simplicity—to cause her to consider the consequences of her *wicked ways*—the place contained nothing besides the cot and a wardrobe with warped doors, but at least it was her own room. She was glad it wasn't so cluttered with useless discarded items that she'd bump into something every time she turned around.

Well, she told herself on a sigh, it wouldn't help matters to sit and bawl over life's injustices. Papa always said it was prayer that changed things. Of course, when it came to Mirah Baxter, one had to wonder if any amount of prayer could change her!

Drawing a fortifying breath, Annora rummaged about for a sheet and flicked it out over the hard mattress. Maybe once there were curtains and a rug it would look somewhat more cheery. This haven might not be so bad after all.

one

Philadelphia, Summer 1878

"Annora, wait." As the departing crowd exited the dark wooden pews and milled toward the church doors after the Sunday service, Lesley Clark leaned around Michael Porter's tall frame, her expressive face aglow. "Will you come to the picnic at Franklin Square next Saturday?"

Just about to vacate the bench where she'd sat with Lesley and several other young people, Annora met her best friend's hopeful smile and hiked a shoulder. "I'm afraid I really can't say just yet."

"Why not?" Michael asked, a merry gleam in his dark brown eyes. "Cousin Jason plans to be there."

Annora fought to quell the stubborn blush that insisted on making an appearance whenever someone made mention of Dr. Markwell's eldest son. Easily the handsomest and most eligible young man among the younger set of Arch Street Church's congregation, his presence within the slightest proximity of hers always caused her pulse to increase—especially since he made no secret of the fact that he sought out her company at gatherings. "Because," she explained for the dozenth time, "you know I have extra duties to tend to at the week's end. I'll have to wait and see if I'm free."

"Oh." Crestfallen, Lesley absently fingered a fold of her striped taffeta skirt.

Annora reached to give her an encouraging pat, noticing as always how much bluer her friend's eyes appeared whenever she wore an ensemble that matched their hue. "Don't despair. I'm quite a fast worker. I'll do my best."

13

"Splendid. Then we'll pray you make it." With a toss of her honey-blond waves, Lesley took her beau's arm, and the pair headed for the vestibule.

Thoughts of the picnic a few days hence made Annora smile as she started toward the back door for home.

❧

Mirah Baxter, peering into the sanctuary from a slim crack in her father's office door, narrowed her eyes and closed the latch without a sound. For two and a half unbearable years, she'd had to put up with that redheaded goody-goody with the unflinching green cat eyes. So she was counting on a picnic, was she? To flaunt herself around Jason Markwell. Well, more's the pity. Mirah had designs on that young man herself. Even if he did happen to be a few years older than she might have preferred. And even if nature did seem to be taking an inordinate amount of time to endow her with measurable charms! She looked scathingly at her girlish body and frowned.

Still, Jason met all of Mother's criteria for a suitable match. All one had to do was get him interested. He seemed partial to sickening sweetness. . .and Mirah knew she was more than accomplished in presenting that sort of face to the world. She would just have to see to it that Annora couldn't quite make this particular outing.

A slow smile teased her lips as her active mind toyed with a few possibilities.

❧

"Phin—e—as!"

Even in the attic with her door closed, Annora heard the blood-chilling shriek clearly. She rolled her eyes and expelled a frustrated breath, incapable of imagining what Mirah had done *this time* that would ultimately be blamed on her. Hardly a fortnight passed without at least one incident of a destructive nature. As it was, Annora had long ago been deprived of even the smallest privilege. When she wasn't helping the housekeeper with the housework or the cooking, or attending service, she was banished to her room. Very seldom was she permitted to leave the grounds unless sent on an errand. How anyone could surmise she somehow managed to find time for mischief despite that fact was beyond her.

Bolstering her courage, she opened the door and tiptoed to the landing in order to ascertain the problem. She could already detect the light pattering of Mirah's footsteps as the younger girl all but flew out of her bedroom and down the stairs. Annora knew she would have to follow soon enough, so she quietly began descending.

"Whatever is amiss, Mother?"

"Look!" Mrs. Baxter wailed. "Just look! Six months of painstaking needlework, all for naught. Why, the entire piece is in tatters. Ruined. Completely ruined. That wretched, ungrateful girl. . ."

"Oh, Mother," Mirah crooned in utmost sympathy, her tone absolutely dripping with honey. "How perfectly awful. Your poor, poor scene. . .and after all your labor every evening."

Annora could just picture the brat's innocent face. No doubt the halo above her head must be dazzling in its brilliance. Why, the dear young thing could do no wrong. Almost choking on the ludicrous farce of it all, Annora held her breath, anticipating how long it would take before she was summoned to face up to this latest alleged infraction.

Barely a heartbeat.

"Annora! Annora Nolan!" the older woman called out. "Come down here this instant!"

"What's happened, Millicent?" the minister inquired, finally arriving at the parlor. "I heard you all the way out in my office."

Descending the main stairs to her certain doom, Annora could see his wife holding forth the tattered embroidery—its myriad strands of colored threads dangling. Obviously it had been savagely hacked to shreds with scissors. She felt a huge lump clog her throat at the horrific sight and swung her attention to Mirah.

The most minuscule gleam of triumph sparked in the frigid brown eyes, then immediately softened with an affected shimmer of moisture as she turned to fawn over her mother.

As Annora proceeded into the parlor, the threesome seared her with the heat of their gazes.

Mrs. Baxter broke the weighty silence. "It positively astounds me, young lady," she said, her clipped words masterfully controlled by what she termed her good breeding, "that you could find it in yourself to be such a constant source of malicious harm to this household."

"I did not do it, madam," Annora whispered.

"Hush!" She shot a glance toward her far-too-meek husband, then directed it at Annora again with a disbelieving shake of her head. "I might have surmised you would resort to falsehood *again*, as you've done so often in the past. In fact, I've come to expect your lies by now. And that, despite all our prayers on your behalf."

"But I did not do it," Annora repeated. "Why would I want to—"

"Precisely!" The control began to wane. "Why *would* you be so ungrateful—so unbelievably *hateful* to people kind enough to take you in when you were homeless and alone in the world? And penniless, I might add, after those less than wise investments your late father made. I must confess, the thought quite boggles my mind. I had hoped, after these tendencies of yours had surfaced when we first took you in, that our dear little Mirah might be a good influence on you. But I see now that I was wrong."

Seeking support from the minister but finding none, Annora felt her last hope fizzle away. She could not bring herself to look at *dear little* Mirah.

"Well, Phineas," the woman continued, her tone one of both resignation and utter defeat, "it should be obvious by now that this. . .ward you insisted we take into our home has far too much idle time on her hands. Some additional labor might be what it will take to cause her to mend her ways. It's high time she assumes the upkeep of the church along with her other duties. Nellie has been feeling overly tired of late. This should serve to alleviate both problems."

Annora could barely swallow.

"Mother," Mirah broke in, cloyingly gracious in her manner. "Perhaps I could help out somehow."

Mrs. Baxter's eyebrows arched high in surprise. "Why, that's very generous of you, darling," she gushed. "But there's no reason why you should trouble yourself over any of this. And I'm afraid your music lessons would suffer were your hands to become roughened by harsh soaps." Her demeanor turned to stone as she regarded Annora once more. "The matter has already been settled."

"Yes. Settled. Ahem." Rocking forward on his toes, then back on his heels, the minister peered through the reading glasses still centered on his nose, his color heightening by the minute. "Well, Miss Nolan, it seems my wife has been gracious enough to extend you yet another chance. I trust you will not waste it. I should hate to be forced to take any more. . . drastic measures. Kindly return to your room. And on the morrow, I shall see you in the sanctuary."

"Yes, sir," Annora all but croaked. "Madam."

On her way to the staircase, she met the housekeeper's expression of understanding as Mrs. Henderson hovered nearby in the hallway. But the level of Annora's misery precluded any comfort from the woman who had grown to be a dear friend. She willed her legs to carry her up to the attic.

Once in her refuge, she lay back on her bed and stared at the rough beams above her head. Only the deep, abiding faith she had in the Lord kept her from hating Mirah Baxter. It would have been an easy enough thing to do, but then the younger girl would have had even more to gloat about if she knew she had turned Annora into a person similar to herself. No, it wouldn't be worth it, when Annora had ammunition of a far superior kind.

She rolled off the bed and onto her knees. *Dearest Father in Heaven, I am supremely thankful for Your presence in my life. If it had not been for You, Mrs. Henderson, and the comfort I find in Mama's Bible every morning, there's no way of knowing what would have become of me. I cannot say I feel any love for Mirah—but I know Your great love extends even to her. Her parents have tried to keep my welfare uppermost in their minds, and I know they've meant well each time they inflicted a new punishment on me. After all, they truly believe I am in the wrong. Who wouldn't fall for that angelic act their spoiled daughter plays to perfection?*

She expelled a slow breath, then continued. *I know Your dear Son faced even more painful betrayal when He walked this earth, and I pray that You will help me to remember how He suffered in silence and how His very life radiated Your infinite love. Please help me to be faithful in following His example.*

Rising to her feet, Annora moved to the window to gaze out upon the rows and rows of rooftops whose varied hues changed colors as the sun moved across the sky. The view was speckled liberally with patches of green grass where laughing, carefree children played. The pleasant scene added to the indescribable peace flooding her being, and Annora smiled. Somehow, some way, even this would work out for her good.

❧

"The cleanin' things are stored in the closet at the end of the hall," Mrs. Henderson explained, escorting Annora about the church building the next day. "I usually look after the reverend's study on Monday mornings, when he goes to visit our shut-ins. Sweepin' and dustin', mostly. Sometimes after a rainy spell you might need to mop. But he don't like anything on his desk disturbed."

"I understand."

The housekeeper exhaled in a huff. "I know I don't have to tell you that the reverend and his wife are good folks at heart," she said gently, placing a hand on Annora's arm. "They made a home for me when my husband passed on and have paid good wages all these years. I wouldn't think of turnin' my back on them. Not even when I'm bone-weary of Mirah and her tempers."

"I know," Annora sighed. "I keep hoping that if I stay long enough, I'll be vindicated, possibly even repay them for their kindnesses. Otherwise, I'd have sought employment with some other family before now."

The older woman appeared to mull over that thought for a moment, then tipped her head. "Still, this is just too much, them pushin' all this work onto those slight shoulders of yours. Why, a good gust of wind could up and whisk you clear into the next county."

"I'm stronger than I look, dear friend," Annora said with a wry smile. She patted the woman's gnarled hand. "And I'm sure I'll catch onto all of this soon enough. What's next?"

Mrs. Henderson continued to regard her for a moment. "I sometimes think you must've been born all growed up. Or else you just had to grow up quicker than most other gals your age—and a far sight more than Little Miss Uppity ever will, I expect!"

Annora could not help but laugh. "I'm just following the example my mother left me. She loved helping people. And now I know why. It brings joy."

"Could be, missy. Could be." Nodding, she started forward again, gesturing toward various rooms as they came to them. "Well, on Tuesdays the ladies get together in this side room and make quilts for the hospital or roll bandages. . .whatever's needed. There's a remnant box in the closet they'll root through. Mostly they bring spare goods from home. After they finish up, around noon, I come back and straighten things a bit. I do whatever other extra rooms look like they need attention through the week."

Annora made a mental note as she listened.

"Of course, the sanctuary gets swept through and dusted toward the end of every week without fail. Mopped at least once a month—sometimes more often near the doors in rainy or snowy weather. On occasion there might be a weddin' or funeral, too. That makes extra work for sure. I'll come help out then. And now and again the reverend likes to have the pews polished. I leave it up to him to say when. Only other thing is the board."

"Board?"

"The public board in the vestibule. A fellow brings by notices to post as they come in from the territories. Sometimes somebody in the congregation wants to rent out a room or sell something. They'll drop a bulletin in the basket for you to pin up. Just keep it lookin' neat, take down the old ones. . . that sort of thing."

"Doesn't sound too awfully hard, really," Annora commented with no little relief. "Spread out through the week the way you've done it."

"Well, all the same, you give a holler if it gets too much for you. I don't mind a'tall lendin' a hand. You've been such a help since you've been here. But. . .be watchful, if you catch my meanin'. Maybe some of the shenanigans will stop now that you'll be so busy. Then again. . ."

Annora gave the housekeeper a hug. "I'll be very, very careful. I promise."

two

After helping the housekeeper bring supper in from the kitchen a few endless days later, Annora took her place opposite Mirah at the table and bowed her head for grace. It never ceased to amaze her that, despite her many alleged offenses, she was expected to dine with the Baxters every evening. But then, she supposed it presented the illusion of family unity, should the odd church member happen by.

". . .in the name of Thy Son, we pray. Amen."

The others echoed the minister's last word, bringing Annora back to the moment at hand, and with supreme effort she opened her eyes.

"It's been the grandest day," Mirah declared, helping herself to a small portion of roasted chicken breast from the platter her father passed her. "But tomorrow will be even better. Just everyone will be at the picnic."

Picnic! Annora had been so busy with her duties, she had completely forgotten about Saturday. And with all that remained to be done to ready the church for Sunday service, she knew she could not even dream of an outing. She seriously doubted she would receive permission anyway, considering the gravity of her latest *transgression*.

"We'll have Annora and Nellie prepare an extra special basket for you, darling," Mrs. Baxter said, subtly quashing Annora's hopes. "There should be plenty of food left over from this evening. Nothing is quite as tasty in a picnic lunch as cold chicken."

"Thank you, Mother. If the weather remains pleasant, I'll wear my new dimity frock." She nibbled delicately at the tender meat on her plate.

21

Annora well knew that the look of relish on the younger girl's face had nothing to do with food, but she maintained her composure, even as her own spirit sank to its lowest ebb. She forced herself to eat as if nothing in the world was wrong, as if her appetite hadn't vanished the instant Mirah opened her mouth. After all, summer wasn't half over, she assured herself. There would be plenty of other social gatherings with Lesley and the other church young people. With Jason. Avoiding the haughty brown eyes across the table, Annora somehow endured the remainder of the interminable meal.

Just as everyone was finishing, the housekeeper entered the room and handed a note to the Reverend Baxter. "This just came for you, sir."

The minister's wife smiled at her. "I must compliment you, Nellie, on this excellent spread. And were those huckleberry tarts I smelled earlier, perchance?"

"Yes, madam."

"Wonderful. I shall have sweet cream on mine, please."

"Well," the reverend cut in, directing his attention to his wife as he laid aside the folded stationery and came to his feet. "I'm afraid I'll have to decline, my dear. I am needed at the Thornby residence right away. It's unlikely I'll be back for several hours. You needn't wait up."

"As you wish." She nodded to Annora. "You may help Nellie serve dessert."

"Yes, ma'am." Blotting her lips on her linen napkin, Annora rose and began clearing the supper plates, glad for the opportunity to leave the room for even a few moments. She was so weary it would be a chore to stay awake until the dishes were done, but no amount of fatigue would stay her tears over the missed outing with her friends.

≈

The interior of the church had never seemed so huge before. Pausing to catch her breath, Annora rested her palms atop the broom handle and gazed at the play of sunlight streaming through the stained glass windows. She had never noticed before how it sparkled over the dust motes in the air, then fell in glowing rainbow patches on the dark polished floor. The gentle peace and reverence of the sanctuary was a balm to her wounded soul as she comforted herself about not seeing Jason Markwell.

She blew a few damp hairs from her eyes and adjusted her kerchief before continuing with the sweeping. Even though the doctor's raven-haired son had never openly declared any special feelings he might have for her, Annora always sensed he enjoyed her presence as much as she did his. Had her absence at today's picnic disappointed him also? Well, she'd probably find out soon enough, when she was forced to suffer through Mirah's embellishments of the occasion over supper. Clenching her teeth, she propped the broom in a corner and pulled a dust rag from the waistband of her apron, then returned to the front.

As she moved between the pulpit and the pump organ in the high-ceilinged room, she heard a woman's muted voice, obviously distressed, drifting from the minister's office.

". . .and he now fears Bertram may not last the night. I don't know what we shall do if he should actually. . .if he—"

"I cannot tell you how sorry I am, my dear Mrs. Thornby," the Reverend Baxter said in his most consoling tone. "He seemed to rally last evening. Of course I will join you and your son as you keep vigil at the bedside."

Feeling the intruder as she eavesdropped on someone's troubles, Annora tiptoed to the opposite end of the large paneled room. She still needed to set the vestibule in order for the morning service, so she made short work of sweeping the enclosed entry.

The sills of the windows flanking either side of the door needed her attention next, she noticed, brushing the rag across their smooth length.

The pastor's door squeaked open just then.

Annora started, and her elbow bumped the small basket off the shelf beneath the public board. Little pieces of paper scattered everywhere even as the Reverend Baxter and his visitor headed toward the vestibule. Quickly gathering the notices within her reach, Annora stuffed them into her apron pockets out of sight, restoring order.

"I'll be along very shortly, Mrs. Thornby," the reverend assured his guest as they reached the exit.

The large-boned woman drew a handkerchief from the wristband of her long sleeve, then pressed it to her nose. "Thank you. Percy and I, we appreciate your prayers and your presence in this hard time. Hester will let you in when you arrive."

Pinning up the new notices during the exchange, Annora saw the pastor nod and close the door behind Mrs. Thornby. Then with little more than a cursory glance at Annora, he went back to his study.

She breathed a sigh of relief. Finished with the last bulletin, she took a last look around, then went to put away her cleaning things. She might be done here, but there was still supper to get.

☙

"And, oh, it was ever so pleasant to stroll in the shade," Mirah gushed as she, her mother, and Annora partook of the evening meal without the reverend. "But best of all was when we paired up for croquet."

"Always a delightful endeavor," Mrs. Baxter said, forking a thin chunk of the roast beef on her plate. "Did you choose a partner, dear?" She raised the meat into her mouth.

Annora toyed with her own food, bracing herself for what she knew would follow.

"I didn't have to, I was chosen. You'll never guess by whom, Mother. It was Dr. Markwell's son, Jason—"

Although Annora thought she was prepared for the news, it still hurt. Little parts of her heart began to shrivel around the edges.

"—and he was ever so gallant, carrying my mallet for me,

seeing to it that I never lacked for lemonade. He was easily the handsomest young man there. And he's quite the wit, as well. I thought I might never stop laughing."

Mrs. Baxter positively glowed. "I couldn't be more pleased, darling. You must do all you can to encourage his attentions. That boy has a splendid future ahead of him, and by the time he finishes studying the practice of medicine, you'll be almost the perfect age to marry. I couldn't think of anyone who would make a finer son-in-law."

It was all Annora could do to force food past the huge lump in her throat.

Later that evening, she couldn't even remember how she had gotten through the remainder of the meal. In the solace of her room at last, while changing into her nightgown, her gaze fell upon her mother's Bible. It was Annora's most treasured possession now—even more dear than the few prized pieces of jewelry Mrs. Henderson had saved from Mama's things. She opened the worn volume to the marker for her habitual daily reading, today in the Thirty-seventh Psalm:

> Fret not thyself because of evildoers, neither be thou envious against the workers of iniquity. For they shall soon be cut down like the grass, and whither as the green herb. Trust in the Lord, and do good; so shalt thou dwell in the land, and verily thou shalt be fed. Delight thyself also in the Lord; and he shall give thee the desires of thine heart. Commit thy way unto the Lord; trust also in him; and he shall bring it to pass.

Her eyes shifted to the window above her bed as she reflected on the passage she had read. It certainly seemed as if at least one evildoer resided at the parsonage, and though Annora didn't exactly wish Mirah *cut down*, it would be rather gratifying to have her be caught in a falsehood once or twice. Then, chagrined at wishing something so bold,

Annora returned to the psalm:

> And he shall bring forth thy righteousness as the
> light, and thy judgment as the noonday. Rest in the
> Lord, and wait patiently for him: fret not thyself
> because of him who prospereth in his way, because of
> the man who bringeth wicked devices to pass. Cease
> from anger, and forsake wrath: fret not thyself in any
> wise to do evil. For evildoers shall be cut off: but those
> that wait upon the Lord, they shall inherit the earth.

I wonder if that could be true for me, Annora mused. *Just
wait patiently, and be exonerated. It's my deepest hope, yet it
seems so unattainable a dream.* Exhaling a ragged breath, she
stood to fold her work clothes for tomorrow.

When she shook out her apron, a small piece of paper
floated to the floor. Curious, Annora picked it up, then recognized it at once as a notice that should have gone up on the
public board:

> *In desperate need. Widower with two small children
> seeks woman to care for same. Duties to include cooking
> and upkeep of home. If the prospect pleases, position
> may lead to matrimony. Travel expenses paid. Reply to
> Lucas Brent, General Delivery, Cheyenne, Wyoming.*

A profound sadness crept over Annora as she read the
announcement over again. Here she was, living in a large city,
where one could easily obtain whatever one required. . .and
feeling sorry for herself! She so seldom gave even the slightest thought to those out in the wild territories who had left
home and family far behind to begin new lives where few
conveniences were available.

With a shake of her head, she breathed a swift prayer of
forgiveness, tacking on a fervent petition for Widower Brent

and his little ones. She'd be sure to pin that notice up on the board tomorrow.

But the burden for the needful little family remained on her heart for a good part of the night.

three

Cheyenne, Wyoming

"Come on, Noah. Put some muscle into it, will you?" Lucas Brent rasped at his dark-haired kid brother as the two of them rocked the stubborn post back and forth. Widening the gate to the corral had been a harder job than he'd anticipated.

"Can't see why we have to get rid of this fool thing anyways," Noah grumbled, swiping his shirt sleeve across his sweaty forehead. He flicked a lock of damp brown hair out of his eyes, then heaved against the wood with all his might. After an almost audible groan, it finally gave, throwing him headlong to the dirt. "Aaaah!"

Lucas had sidestepped just in time. He smirked and offered a hand to his sibling, then tugged him to his feet. "I didn't want it there, that's why."

"Don't know what difference it makes," Noah groused, sweeping a scathing glance down his now-dusty shirtfront. He brushed himself off and wiped his hands on his jeans. "Can we call it quits now?"

"There's lots of daylight left."

"Man, all you want to do anymore is work! I'm tired. It's hot. And it's been a long day."

"Well," Lucas said with a shrug, "looks like there might be a storm coming. Go on. I'm gonna keep at it for a bit."

Noah's youthful features relaxed, and his blue eyes shone with relief as he turned and strode past the barn.

"Hey, check on the girls," Lucas called after him. "Make sure they aren't into something they shouldn't be. I'll be along soon."

"Sure." Whistling now, the young man lengthened his strides toward the four-room clapboard dwelling a short distance away.

Lucas watched him go, noting how his brother's once-skinny frame was muscling out since he'd come out to Wyoming in hopes of finding adventure. Seemed to be mellowing a little, too. The hard work was curbing some of the mischievous bent he'd acquired growing up in Denver. But would the kid ever settle down? Contemplating the unlikely possibility, Lucas inflated his lungs and slowly let the air out as he began filling the hole the extracted post had left behind.

Oh, well, he should be thankful to get *any* help out of that daydreaming nineteen-year-old. Noah showed little regard for the never-ending amount of chores that needed doing on a farm. One of these days somebody should give him a good—

A joyous, high-pitched shriek cut into his musings. Straightening to ease a kink in his back, Lucas swung a glance in the direction of the house just as his little daughters, Melinda and Amy, scampered out onto the weathered front porch. He smiled to himself. It was good to hear them starting to act like youngsters again. They'd been far too withdrawn since the funeral, hardly ever giggling like they used to.

But dwelling on the relentless ache inside him since Francie's death would only worsen it. With a sigh, he turned his focus to the task at hand and tamped the loose earth into place.

"Papa! I'm hungry," towheaded Amy hollered from the yard.

"Isn't it getting suppertime? The sun is low," her big sister pointed out with six-year-old logic.

"Yeah, I'm coming." Gathering his tools, Lucas headed for the barn.

The pair met him halfway and skipped hand in hand alongside, Amy's long blond hair feathering in the breeze. Lucas noticed it wasn't nearly as shiny as it had been when their mama had kept after it. But the braids he'd put in Melinda's deep brown locks were holding up pretty well, if he did say so himself.

"Melinda found a hurt birdie," Amy said, eyes the same azure shade as Francie's shining up at him. "Uncle Noah says it's gonna die. Is it, Papa?"

"I don't know, pumpkin. I'll have to see how bad it's been hurt."

"I hope it doesn't die," Melinda said on a sad sigh, her lips turning down at the corners. She fingered a new tear in her dress.

"Did God put birdies in Heaven?" Amy asked.

Lucas grimaced. He had stopped giving much thought to heavenly affairs the day Francie had been laid to rest. . .when it dawned on him that the Almighty didn't seem overly concerned about two innocent little ones who now had to grow up without their mother. But he smiled gently and squeezed her little shoulder with his free hand. "Well—"

"Course there's birds in Heaven, silly," her sibling announced. "Birds are pretty. And Heaven has all pretty things. Mama told us that, remember? When we looked in the picture book."

The sweet remembrance crimped Lucas's midsection, and he found it hard to respond. But they had reached the barn entrance, and as usual, the girls made a beeline for the stall housing Chesapeake, his sorrel-colored stallion. Parking his gear with the rest of the tools, Lucas watched them petting and cooing over the sorrel-colored bay while he checked to be sure Noah had fed the animal.

"Come on, you two," he said, offering each a hand. "Let's go get supper going."

"Hooray!" the girls chorused, each trying to be first to grab hold.

Their sweet smiles were a pleasure to see. . .even against those dirt-streaked faces. A person didn't have to look too close to concede that both girls could use a decent bath tonight. And once they were tucked into bed, he'd make good use of the water himself. If he hunted hard enough, he might even find some clean clothes somewhere, too. If not, reasonably clean would have to do.

"What're we gonna eat?" Melinda asked.

Lucas had been wondering the same thing himself. The long hours of work it took to keep his mind too occupied to feel sorry for himself precluded any kind of involved meal. "Did you two bring in the eggs today?"

"Uh huh." Amy scrunched up her face. "But we had eggs last night. And yesterday at dinner."

"And beans and ham almost every other day," his older daughter reminded him.

"Well, how about pancakes?" Lucas offered. "You like those."

"You mean, every day?" Melinda challenged.

"No, sweetheart. Just tonight. For special."

She nodded. "All right. Pancakes."

"All right," he said as they neared the house. "Wash up, then, while I get them going." He gave one of Melinda's braids a gentle tug. "Help Amy do a good job, huh?"

"Sure, Papa. Come on, Sissy. You can be first."

The girls went to dip water from the rain barrel into the wash basin that sat on the low table next to it, and Lucas continued on into the house.

Barely through the open doorway, he shook his head and turned his eyes upward. Only four rooms, and nothing but clutter from one to the next—while Noah, oblivious to it all, lounged on the sofa in the front room, one leg hooked over the arm, his bare foot dangling.

Lucas glared at him on the way to the stove. "Wouldn't hurt you to pick up a little once in awhile, you know."

Noah snorted and closed the Sears Roebuck catalog he'd been flipping through. "Why? It'll only get messed up again. Besides, nobody sees it but us."

"No excuse. This isn't how you were raised."

"Yeah, well, Ma and Pa ain't gonna swoop down here with their harps to yell at me no more, are they? It ain't my idea to work my head off all day every day, like you're so set on doing since Francie died. I put in my share outside. I shouldn't have to keep it up when the day's done."

"Is that right?" Lucas replied, looking askance at him.

"Yep. That's the way I see it."

"Well, the way *I* see it, it's time you grew up and took on some responsibility. Show some appreciation for having a roof over your head."

"Plenty of time for that." Noah came to his feet. "Right now, I think I'll ride on into town."

"I told you a storm's on the way."

"So? A few drops of rain never hurt anybody. I need to see a cheerful face for a change. Might even run into Postmaster Cummings while I'm there. He'd know if there's been an answer to the notice you sent east with the circuit rider." He jammed his bare feet into his boots and tromped out the door.

But Lucas knew it was way too soon to hope for answers.

❧

Almost every member of Arch Street Church must have come to Mr. Thornby's funeral yesterday, Annora deduced. At least that's how the floor looked, tramped from front to back with mud from the heavy rain. And with this being Mrs. Henderson's baking and laundry day, Annora knew she would have to handle this task on her own. She blew some stray hairs out of her eyes with a disgusted huff, then went to get the bucket and scrub brush.

Knowing she was going to be at it for hours, she decided to start back at the door, where it looked the worst, then work her way toward the front. She rolled up her sleeves and began the tedious chore.

Annora had finished the length of one side and had gotten to the middle of the other when she first detected faint voices coming from the pastor's office, its door typically ajar during the warmer months. Not particularly prone to eavesdropping on matters that didn't concern her, Annora was rather glad the conversation could not be heard over the noise of the scrub brush. But when she switched to the rinse rag, short snatches could be heard quite distinctly, so she tried to concentrate on her work rather than listening.

". . .but for that will. I had no idea it existed."

"He might not have been thinking clearly, my dear Mrs. Thornby. The stipulation was likely due to his illness, I'm sure."

"That's not what Lawyer Sherman tells me. He is convinced Bertram was in his right mind to the end."

Dipping the brush into the suds once more, Annora scrubbed another portion of the floor around her, then wrung out the rinse rag to wipe up the soap and dirty water.

"But marriage!" The woman cried. "To attach such a condition to Percy's inheritance. Bad enough for us to be left alone so suddenly—but that!"

Annora couldn't resist chuckling inwardly. Percival Thornby? Get married? A picture of the paunchy young man with sallow skin flashed in her mind. His forehead had already laid claim to all the territory up to the middle of his scalp—and him no more than twenty-five. Worse yet, he mirrored many of his mother's irritating gestures and voice inflections. He had turned his simpering affections in the direction of nearly every unmarried girl at church at one time or another, without getting a single taker. In fact, it was rather a joke among them that such a sissy would never find gumption enough to leave his doting mother in the first place!

Nevertheless, she couldn't help but remember how sad it felt to part with a member of one's family. Whispering a prayer of comfort for the newly bereaved church folk, Annora took the brush again and began the next section. Rinsing it, she let her thoughts drift to Jason Markwell and his enticing manliness.

"Now, now, my good woman," the minister said soothingly. "Your concern might be premature. Let's pray about the matter and leave it in God's hands. Meanwhile, put your mind at rest. I'll see what I can find out about it from your lawyer and call on you the moment I have anything to report."

"If you think there's hope," she said hesitantly, her own tone evidence of her doubt.

Standing to her feet, Annora picked up the heavy water bucket and moved to the next area.

The voices grew fainter momentarily, an indication that Reverend Baxter had shown the widow out the side exit. Expecting complete silence after that, Annora was startled to hear the minister's wife speak directly after the report of his footsteps indicated his return.

"Well. I must say, that is about the strangest thing I have ever heard. Didn't it strike you as such, Phineas?"

He grunted in response. "Just remember, it was related in strictest confidence. It is not to go beyond these walls."

"Of course. But my heart goes out to the poor woman. She's beside herself. There must be something we can do to help."

Annora picked up the brush to rewet it.

"Well," she heard the minister say, "there are a number of young women in our congregation who are of marriageable age. Edna Morris, for one. Violet Biddle and her sister Iris." He paused. "And do not discount the younger set—Lesley Clark and her circle."

The brush slipped from Annora's grasp and plunged into the murky scrub water. Retrieving it, she resumed her chore.

"Phineas. . ."

Something in Mrs. Baxter's tone made Annora freeze in place, sudsy droplets plopping from the bristles to the floor. She sat back on her heels, a deep foreboding pressing upon her chest.

"You know," the woman went on in a confidential tone, "this might just be an answer to our prayers."

four

An answer to prayer? Mrs. Baxter's remark sank like a rock to the bottom of Annora's heart. She had a dreadful suspicion what the answer to those prayers might be. . .or rather, *whom*. A ward was, after all, expendable.

More rational thoughts took over. No sense jumping to conclusions when her fears might be entirely ungrounded. With her pulse throbbing in her ears, she kept absolutely still, straining to hear more.

"What do you mean, Millicent?" came the pastor's voice.

"Well," his wife explained quietly, "think of our dilemma. Of the *incidences* that have occurred in our own home over the past two years."

A short pause. "You're referring to Annora."

"Of course."

The slender thread of hope to which Annora had clung snapped, and a heaviness like nothing she had ever experienced pressed the very breath from her. Fearing that her guardians might inadvertently glance into the sanctuary and discover their conversation was anything but private, she crept silently out of the line of view. She stooped down behind a plant table near the front corner, longing desperately for the discussion to end.

"Much as I rue having to admit failure with that girl," the older woman went on, "I fear we've no other choice. Rather than showing common gratitude for the refuge provided her in time of dire need, she has chosen to inflict us with malicious harm. Time and again. And I, for one, have reached my limit with her."

"Still," the pastor reasoned, "there's much to consider here.

I shouldn't want to make a decision in haste."

"Haste! Is that what you deem it—when what we must consider above all else is our own daughter's welfare? I dare say, while we sit by waiting for Mirah's excellent character to make even the slightest impression on the girl, the very opposite could be happening. I could not bear it if our own darling child were to be corrupted by the likes of her."

"Hm. I see your point—however unlikely it is. I'll mention the possible solution to the Widow Thornby when next I call on her."

"This opportunity comes straight from God's hand, Phineas," Mrs. Baxter murmured. "I truly feel it."

"Yes, well, unless the widow and her son are receptive to the suggestion, there's no point in mentioning it to anyone just yet. Most especially not Annora."

"I agree. I'll not say a word."

"Good. Well, I have some calls to make, my dear. I'll escort you over to the parsonage."

Seconds later, the closing of the side door echoed hollowly through the building.

Annora felt utterly empty, utterly alone. She sank slowly to the floor in silent misery, the tears inside her trapped somewhere between anguish and despair. What had she done to deserve such punishment? Would the Lord truly allow such a fate to befall her?

Even hours later, the ache remained. The church had once again been set to rights, ready for the next service. Annora had beaten the Persian rug from the parlor free of dust and polished Mrs. Baxter's silver tea service to a satin sheen. As she replaced her soiled work apron with a fresher one up in her attic room, her wrist brushed against the pocket, bringing a faint crackle of paper. *The unposted notice*—still awaiting a prominent place on the public board! If it weren't for her forgetfulness, someone might have seen it and applied for the position by now!

Annora gave fleeting thought to the possibility of writing to the widower herself, then just as quickly rejected the idea. After all, if a man were desperate enough to advertise for a wife, he must be even worse than Percival Thornby!

The uncharitable thoughts pricked her conscience. She really must remember to take that bulletin with her next time she went to the church! Tossing it on the stand beside the bed, she hastened downstairs to help with supper.

"You seem a little off today," Mrs. Henderson remarked a short while later, quartering the potato Annora had just peeled. She dropped the cut vegetable into the pot of stew bubbling atop the coal range. "Something troubling you, honey?"

Annora manufactured a smile. "I'm a little tired." It was by no means a lie, but neither was it the whole truth. She just didn't trust herself to elaborate on something which—hopefully—might turn out to be of no consequence. Time enough for that if her worst fears were confirmed. Percival Thornby might not accept the Baxters' proposition.

"I'm sure you are," the kind woman crooned. "And sorry I was that you were left with the whole sanctuary to do after that big funeral."

"No matter. It's finished now." She rinsed another potato in the bowl of water and handed it to the housekeeper, then started on the carrots. But having been reminded of Lucas Brent and his troubles, mere moments before, her mind drifted to the matter several times as she continued supper preparations. Perhaps someone in another church had responded to the widower's plea, and soon he would have the help he so desperately needed. She prayed so.

❧

". . .and Mr. Montclair said I'd played a wonderful rendition of the piece," Mirah boasted proudly, taking a second warm roll from the basket and breaking off a small section. She dipped it in her stew, then popped it into her mouth.

"Why, that's splendid, darling," her mother gushed. "I'm gratified that your talents merit the dear price we pay for the man's instruction."

Only vaguely listening to the chatter over the mealtime tinkle of silverware and china, Annora took a sip of water from her goblet. As she did, she caught a peculiar look pass between the minister and his wife, and a sickening dread erased the limited appetite she had brought to the supper table.

Mirah, however, seemed blissfully unaware of the underlying current of tension Annora felt as keenly as a toothache. "He has ordered a new collection of minuets and concertos for me to master," the younger girl went on, her brown eyes sparkling. "If I learn them well enough, he says I might be invited to play in the next recital at the conservatory! And only a select few of his outside students are extended that honor, Mother." Her long, tapered finger flicked a shining ringlet behind her shoulder.

"How wonderful, my dear," her father commented. "However, do rest assured that whether or not an invitation to play at the conservatory ensues, your mother and I are very proud of you."

"Indeed." Giving her daughter's hand a few loving pats, Mrs. Baxter then rang a tiny silver bell, signaling for dessert.

Annora stood at once and began collecting dinner plates and bowls. Rounding the head of the table, she reached to remove the pastor's dishes.

"Thank you," he said in customary politeness, but his demeanor appeared troubled. He cleared his throat. "Later this eve, after you've finished helping Nellie, Mrs. Baxter and I would like a word with you, Annora. In my study."

"Yes, sir," she managed, purposely refraining from meeting Mirah's curious expression. And worse, his wife averted her gaze entirely. Annora's insides began to quiver. *Please, Heavenly Father, don't let it be what I think it is. I could not bear that.* But inside, she knew the plea was in vain.

❧

Annora found the older couple waiting for her when she finally succeeded in forcing her legs to carry her to the study. The room, with its rich assortment of books lining the built-in shelves, had grown quite familiar to her since she'd begun dusting and sweeping it regularly. But on this visit the scent of the leather bindings she had once found so pleasant seemed cold and acrid. The very atmosphere was heavy and unwelcoming.

"Come in, child," the reverend said calmly. "And close the door, if you will." His small frame seemed dwarfed behind his massive carved desk.

Noting Mrs. Baxter's rigid posture in a Queen Anne side chair, hands folded in the lap of her somber afternoon ensemble, Annora could scarcely will her trembling fingers to make the latch function. But as the click echoed in the room, she drew a ragged breath and straightened her spine, then turned to face her guardians.

"Sit down, please," the minister said, gesturing toward a vacant chair near the desk.

As always, she obeyed.

"I'll come right to the point," he continued. "You are aware, of course, that a prominent member of our congregation has passed away."

"Yes," she whispered.

"Well, it seems the late Mr. Thornby left his loved ones in somewhat of a quandary. Through an unusual stipulation inserted in his most recent will, it seems his only son and heir, Percival, is prohibited from claiming his rightful inheritance for many years unless he marries before his next birthday. . . which, as it happens, is less than a month away."

Only with supreme effort was Annora able to remain dutifully in her seat. The compulsion to flee the room, her guardians, and the house was all she could imagine as a way out of this horrible predicament. Her throat tightened. "I–I fail to see what that has to do with me," she stammered.

"On the contrary, my dear," Mrs. Baxter said evenly, her aloof hazel eyes suddenly focused directly on Annora, "it would quite surprise me if you did not have some inkling regarding the decision my husband and I have made, as well as your personal involvement in the matter."

A huge mass of fear clogged Annora's throat.

"We have approached Percival Thornby and his mother with what we feel is a solution to a number of problems. Ours and theirs," the Reverend Baxter announced.

"Please," Annora begged, looking from the man to his wife, then back again. "Please, don't tell me I—"

"Oh, do not resort to useless entreaties," his wife piped in. "It has been obvious to us from the very first that you have been anything but grateful we took you into our home."

"But that's not true—"

Mrs. Baxter raised a hand to silence her. "Regardless of your denials, I fear your actions have spoken far more blatantly than anything you might try to say now. Let me assure you that for some time I have been on the verge of complete and utter despair over your spiteful deeds. For such an opportunity to arise now in order to benefit the lot of us, it can only have come from the Almighty's own hand."

"You do happen to be of marriageable age," the reverend explained before Annora could respond. "And for us, your legal guardians, to be able to arrange such an advantageous match for you is an answer to prayer. We can rest in knowing you will be comfortably taken care of. The Thornby wealth is considerable. If our Mirah wasn't so young, we would not hesitate a bit in securing such a splendid match for her."

"But. . .but I. . .can't—"

The older woman's obvious impatience began to assert itself. "We did not call you in here to ask your opinion of the matter," she stated firmly. "Only to inform you that your marriage to young Mr. Thornby has been agreed upon and will proceed as swiftly as we are able to arrange it. Naturally, as our ward, we desire you to have a beautiful wedding not unlike we intend for our dear Mirah one day. These plans, of course, will take some doing, on such short notice. But that is our concern, not yours."

"I shall post the banns at once," her husband went on.

"And I shall schedule your first fitting for your bridal gown and trousseau on the morrow," Mrs. Baxter added.

Annora could only stare in mute defeat. They weren't interested in her opinion. They didn't care how she might feel about having her whole future handed to someone she loathed. And their dear sweet Mirah. . .Annora could just imagine the triumphant gloating she'd have to endure from that one!

"In view of the nearness of your upcoming nuptials, Annora," Mrs. Baxter said, cutting into her bitter musings, "we shall, of course, relieve you of some of your duties. We wouldn't want you to appear taxed when the day of your wedding arrives."

Stunned and shocked as she was over the fate awaiting her, the pronouncement of less work carried not even the slightest comfort. Annora could not manage any kind of utterance. The older couple regarded her steadily as if she should consider this the happiest news ever delivered.

"You may go to your room now," the minister finally said. "I'm sure you need time to thank our blessed Lord for this most fortunate turn of events. And tomorrow evening, we will invite your betrothed to supper. It's only proper that the two of you become better acquainted in the scant time remaining before you two are united in marriage."

"Our Mirah will be so pleased for you," her mother breathed.

With that understatement ringing in her ears, Annora rose with as much dignity as she could muster, her quaking legs barely able to support her as she stumbled to the door and mounted the stairs to her sanctuary in the attic.

And all the way up, she hoped she would die in her sleep.

Collapsing on her bed, she drew her knees to her chest and lay shivering in her misery, her glance drifting idly about the small quarters. Her gaze came to a dead halt when it fell upon the forgotten notice still awaiting its prominent position on the public board.

Annora bolted upright and snatched it from her bedside table. Heart pounding, she unfolded the handwritten bulletin and read it over again.

A housekeeper. She'd had sufficient qualifications there.

Someone to care for two small children. Well, no actual experience, but Mama had often remarked that a child who was kept clean and fed was a happy child.

If the prospect pleases, position could lead to matrimony.

In this case, she would at least be given a choice. And surely, whoever this Lucas Brent was, he couldn't be any worse than that mama's boy, Percival Thornby. Could he?

Annora rooted through a discarded lap desk she'd discovered some weeks ago and removed paper and a quill, praying that her letter and Mr. Brent's returning answer would reach their destinations before the dreaded day.

five

In her newest, most fashionable jade taffeta gown, her red-gold tresses a mass of ringlets intertwined with ribbons, Annora grudgingly answered the summons to join the Baxters and her intended in the parsonage's luxurious parlor.

Percival Thornby rose and met her in the doorway as she approached. "Ah. Miss Nolan," he wheezed. "I've been anticipating the opportunity to dine with you this evening."

"Mr. Thornby," she managed, with a slight dip of her head as she smothered her displeasure.

He reached for her hand and bowed ceremoniously over it. Thankfully, however, he did not kiss it but escorted her to the indigo brocade settee and seated her. He took the opposite side.

A brief uncomfortable period followed, during which no one looked at anyone for more than a split second. Finally the Reverend Baxter resumed the polite conversation Annora's arrival had obviously interrupted.

Tongue-tied amid the drone of voices, she disregarded them completely, maintaining her composure by sheer determination. She could not help noticing how the waistcoat of Percival's black silk suit strained across the broad expanse of his belly as he leaned back against the cushions. And the collar of his shirt had been starched so crisply he appeared to have no neck at all.

Annora shifted her position and tried to focus on the contrast between the heavy furnishings and some of the exquisite porcelain figurines adorning the room. Anything to keep her mind and eyes elsewhere. From time to time she would become aware of Percival Thornby's admiring glances, and her color heightened along with her discomfort. This evening was destined to last forever.

But she could not dismiss the expression on her intended's flushed face. . .a mixture of incredulity and satisfaction at having been granted a hitherto unattainable prize. And something about the way he looked at Annora made her feel undressed. She studied her hands, tightly clasped in her lap to keep them still.

"I'm ready to serve supper, madam," Mrs. Henderson finally announced from the doorway.

Everyone rose. But before Annora could take a step, Percival tipped his head politely and offered his arm. She forced a smile and placed her fingers lightly atop his smooth sleeve. At least in the dining room, eating would consume part of the time, and she would have a valid excuse not to join the inane chatter.

"And what are your future goals, Percival?" the Reverend Baxter asked, after everyone had been seated and the blessing pronounced. He handed the platter of roast pork to their guest.

The fleshy young man altered his position self-consciously on the chair. "Goals. Ahem." He helped himself to several generous slices of meat. "I suppose," he announced in his high-pitched lisp, "I'll be doing my utmost to look after the two women in my life. I haven't thought beyond that."

Two women. Annora cringed inwardly at having been thrown upon the Thornby household merely as a means to save the inheritance. She could only surmise how the recently widowed matriarch would view the presence of a usurper to her son's attention.

Detecting Mirah's barely visible smirk as the dark-haired girl took a sip of water from her goblet, Annora felt the last remnants of hunger vanish. Normally she would have devoured the sumptuous fare, but tonight the sight and smell of serving dishes heaped high with the housekeeper's fine cooking only made her stomach churn. She accepted the platter Percy was passing to her and took the smallest slice possible. He, however, scooped a veritable mountain of mashed potatoes onto his plate and sampled a forkful.

"Are you planning a wedding trip?" Mirah asked him, her lips twitching with restrained mirth.

"Trip. Ah." Percy swallowed and blotted his mouth on his napkin. "Actually, Miss Nolan and I have not yet discussed her wishes along that line. Mother and I are making arrangements to set aside a six-week period for travel. Naturally, we will be only too happy to escort my new bride anywhere she desires."

Annora's heart plummeted as everyone turned to her, awaiting a response. All she could think of was how very little effort it would take to be sick, right here, in front of them all.

❧

Lucas listened idly to the jingle of the harness as Jethro and Rex, his workhorses, plodded homeward from town in the growing dusk.

"How much farther, Papa?" Melinda asked, standing up in the bed of the wagon and clutching the seat back. "I have to go."

"Me, too," Amy piped in at her side.

"Didn't you go with Miss Rosemary to the outhouse, like I told you, while I was getting the supplies?" he chided his older daughter gently.

"Yes, Pa, but then she took us to the well and let us turn the crank. She let us have a big drink of cold water from the bucket. Now we have to go again."

"Okay, okay." Rolling his eyes, Lucas released a long, slow breath and drew in on the reins. "There are some bushes over there," he indicated with his head. "Be quick about it."

"Yes, Papa," the youngsters chorused. Hopping down from the wagon, they bolted happily out of sight.

Waiting for the girls to return, Lucas reached for the mail he'd picked up in town and sifted through it one more time, carefully, just in case there had been a letter from back East that he hadn't noticed. But no such luck. Maybe there'd never be an answer.

He set aside the items from the post office and let his thoughts drift to Rosemary Evans, the comely milliner whose small bonnet shop was becoming more and more a lucrative enterprise with the growth of Cheyenne. Though fetching enough to turn any number of heads, the hatmaker showed no inclination to marry at the moment. . .at least, not a widower who'd been "saddled," as she'd termed it, with two children.

Lucas suspected that if he'd been left completely alone, however, flaxen-haired Rosemary would have been first in line to pick up the pieces of his life. She'd all but come right out and said it over refreshments she'd served when he'd gone by her place to pick up the badly needed mending she'd been kind enough to do for him. No, best not to entertain fantasies about a lady who was more interested in making her fortune than she was in being mama to a pair of little girls that weren't hers.

His musings came to an abrupt end with the sound of giggles and pattering footsteps as his daughters scrambled aboard the wagon again. Flicking the reins over the horses' backs, Lucas clucked his tongue. "Come on, boys. Let's get on home."

❧

Annora stepped behind the folding screen to dress. Tired after standing motionless on the dressmaker's fitting stool for most of the afternoon, she circled her head slowly, trying to relieve her stiff neck. Then she removed her petticoats from the wall pegs and began pulling them on.

"Let me know when you need help fastening buttons," Gertie Simms, the bubbly assistant called out.

"Thank you, I will." But less than anxious to return to the parsonage just yet, Annora continued her leisurely movements. The Baxters had spared no expense in providing her with a lovely trousseau. Indeed, under any other circumstances, Annora would have been in seventh heaven at the very thought of possessing such a glorious wardrobe. But although her guardians truly believed they were acting in her best interest, such an unwanted marriage made Annora's very skin crawl. She was taxed to maintain a pleasant demeanor in their presence. There had to be some way of forestalling her union with the heir to the Thornby estate. A miraculous intervention by God. *Please, Dear Father, don't let this happen to me.*

"Ready?" Gertie asked, peeking around the screen, her bright blue eyes alight with friendliness.

"Yes." With a thin smile, Annora turned her back to the nimble-fingered brunette who appeared only a couple years older than herself.

"La, what a pretty wardrobe you'll be wearin'," Gertie said breathlessly, slipping each pearl button on Annora's dress through its corresponding loop. "Your missus chose all the newest fabrics from France and laces from Belgium. So elegant, they are, to work on."

"Yes. And I'm surprised at how quickly you're finishing everything," Annora said with fatal acceptance. No one seemed to care that her whole future was spinning out of control.

"Well, my mistress has all us girls sewin' past closin' to fill the order. She'd have our heads if it was our fault that a grand weddin' got held up!" Chuckling to herself, the slim girl straightened and stepped away. "There. Now, a few more fittin's an' you'll not be seein' the likes of us again for awhile."

"I've enjoyed getting to know you and the others," Annora admitted truthfully. "Especially you, Gertie. I hope your mother continues to gain strength."

"Thanks, miss. It's been a help, my earnin' good money here. Little by little, the Good Lord supplies what she needs."

"Yes. Well, I'll see you tomorrow afternoon, then. Do have a pleasant day." Smiling, Annora crossed through the cluttered workroom. The small silver bell jangled in its bracket above the entrance as she exited.

Late afternoon sunshine cast long shadows between the red brick buildings lining either side of Market Street. The coolness of the shady spots felt welcome to Annora's feet as she traipsed along the edge of the cobbled road. Grateful that no one had accompanied her today, she gave in to the impulse to pop in on her best friend from church. The bakery Lesley's parents owned was barely two blocks out of her way.

As she neared the squat one-story building tucked between a leather shop and a printing business, the tantalizing aroma of fresh baked goods grew stronger. The overhead bell sounded as she opened the door and went inside.

"Well, well," Lesley said, looking up from behind the wide counter, her rosy lips widening with a smile. "A friendly face. Always a welcome sight." She wiped her hands on the long apron covering her work dress and came to hug Annora. "What brings you by?"

"Mostly I needed to see a friendly face myself," Annora admitted glumly as the embrace ended and they parted.

"Why? Whatever is wrong? Are the Baxters working you too hard—as usual?"

"You haven't heard?"

"Heard what? I've been up at Wind Gap at my auntie Edna's for the past ten days, remember? I just got home last evening."

At the look of puzzled concern on Lesley's expressive features, Annora felt her own eyes fill with tears. "Oh, Les. You have no idea what's happened. It's just dreadful."

"What is?" Reaching for Annora's hand, Lesley clutched it in both of hers, her delicate brows dipping into a vee above her clear blue eyes. "Oh, do tell me what has you in such a state."

Still struggling to contain her emotions, Annora drew a stabilizing breath. "I–I'm to be. . .married." Then the floodgates let loose, and she collapsed, weeping, into her dear friend's comforting arms.

The slender honey-blond crooned softly as she patted Annora's back. "I don't understand. How can that be?"

"They—they want to. . .get rid of m—me," Annora sobbed.

"Why, I've never heard anything so horrid," Lesley said consolingly. "But—whom will you marry?"

Annora couldn't bring herself to answer. Inside, a part of her still clung to the hope that she'd awaken from this nightmare. . .that unless she actually uttered the truth aloud, it wouldn't be real.

"Who is it, Annora?" her friend probed gently.

"I—I don't even w—want to say his n—name." It took two tries before she managed to force it past her lips. "It's—it's *Percival Thornby*!" The announcement spewed forth on a croaking whisper.

Lesley's breath caught in her throat, and she clutched Annora all the more tightly, stroking her hair as the sobs continued.

How much time passed, Annora could not even guess. But when her tears began to subside, she sniffed and eased away, drying her cheeks on a handkerchief from her pocket. She had only a fragile hold on her control, and she knew if she dared to meet her friend's sympathetic gaze, she would break down again.

"There's only one thing to do. You must run away," Lesley declared adamantly.

"Where could I go?"

"I don't know yet. But I'll think of someplace, I promise."

Annora finally raised her lashes and searched Lesley's face. The sight of the determination displayed there bolstered her courage. "Well, the truth is, I've applied for a position out in the Wyoming Territory. . .a housekeeper and nursemaid."

"Are you serious?"

With a nod, Annora sighed. "I haven't told anyone. But

there hasn't been time to hear if I've been accepted for the post. Someone else may have already been selected."

Lesley did not respond.

"That position might also involve marriage."

The look that passed between them held a raft of unspoken implications, but Lesley was considerate enough not to press the matter. "When is the, um, wedding here supposed to take place?"

Annora grimaced. "Sometime before Percy's next birthday, two weeks away. . .the very moment all the plans have been finalized. I'm returning now from a fitting for my gown and trousseau," she continued in a rush before another wave of tears swamped her. "I've never possessed such lovely, elegant things. The Baxters truly think they're doing me a favor— and, of course, Mirah's absolutely jumping with glee. You cannot imagine."

"This is all pretty grim," Lesley agreed. "But perhaps you'll hear from Wyoming before then. . .not that I wish to part with my bosom friend, you understand."

"I hardly think there's time, Les. Everything is progressing so quickly."

"That may very well be," Lesley said with conviction. "But I'm not about to stand by and do nothing while your whole life is thrown to the vultures. This wedding will not take place. You'll see. Somehow, some way, we'll come up with something. Some way out."

six

In her room, early that evening, Annora heard the bell pull announce the arrival of a visitor downstairs. Shortly afterward, light footsteps sounded on the steps, pausing briefly on the second floor before continuing on to the attic.

Annora sat up on her bed, and her questioning glance caught her best friend's pretty smile at the door.

"May I come in?" Lesley asked breathlessly.

"Of course." Annora patted the coverlet beside herself.

Lesley stepped inside and crossed the room, a small wrapped package in her hands. "I brought you something. . . so Mrs. Baxter wouldn't feel it odd that I came."

"You've always been clever," Annora teased as she accepted the gift. Smiling, she unwrapped the brown paper. Her heart contracted at the sight of a pair of fine batiste pillow slips. "Oh, Les," she murmured, fingering the embroidered hems edged with handmade lace. "How beautiful. But these are things you've made for yourself, for the day you become a bride."

"Well, yes. But I wanted to give you something special, so when you're an old married lady you won't forget the girl who was once your dearest friend."

"You'll always be my dearest friend," Annora assured her with a hug. "Married or not." Then, drawing away, she grew serious. "But if the gift was only a pretext, what is the real reason for your visit?"

Lesley rose and tiptoed to close the door. "I don't want anyone to overhear us," she whispered, returning to her seat.

"Why? What's happened?"

"Nothing. I've just been so consumed with worry for you,

51

I wanted to find out if there'd been any word from Wyoming yet."

Annora shook her head soberly. "And I'd hate to surmise what would happen if something should arrive on a day when I'm not the one who picks up the household mail. I'd be called to account for such a scandalous act. Besides, in truth, I'm not completely sure that's a better fate than what awaits me here."

"Well, I dare say, it can hardly be worse!" Lesley exclaimed.

Annora conceded inwardly that her friend was likely right.

"What will you do if there's no response?"

"I'm trying not to dwell on that."

A conspiratorial expression drew Lesley's fine brows together. "Well, I'll tell you what I would do, were I in your shoes."

"Oh? And what might that be, if I dare ask?"

"I would go anyway."

The announcement hung suspended between them for a timeless moment. Then Annora shook her head. "How could I, Les? How? It's possible that Mr. Brent has already hired someone else, you know. But even if he hasn't, I've no idea of the price of a fare west, much less where I'd obtain traveling funds for such a journey. Then there's the small matter of sneaking a trunk packed with clothes out of the house, to say nothing of lugging it all those blocks to the railroad station without anyone noticing." She paused to take a breath, trying to convince herself a single one of those thoughts she had entertained was even feasible. "And even if by some miracle I could somehow manage all those things, the very idea of going so far by myself is–is. . ."

"Shh." Lesley put a comforting hand on Annora's shoulder. "All of that, as my mother is so fond of saying, 'is difficult, but not impossible.' First things first. The money."

Her curiosity sparked, Annora met the confident gaze.

"Didn't you tell me that Mrs. Henderson salvaged a few pieces of your mother's jewelry?"

"Well, yesss. . ." Annora hedged. "But how could I part with those? It's all I have left of Mama's."

Lesley nodded in understanding as she toyed with one of her shiny blond curls. "But consider the alternative, Nora. Would you rather have the jewelry and go through with your wedding to Percy? Or could you put those sentiments aside and accept your mother's help? I'm sure she wouldn't want you to settle for a lifetime of unhappiness. Would she?"

Annora could not even respond. What she needed most was time to reason things out. Time to pray.

"Come by the shop again after tomorrow's fitting. We'll go together to inquire about a railroad ticket."

"I can't promise," Annora confessed. "But I will try."

"It doesn't cost anything to ask, you know," her friend urged softly.

At the sound of approaching footsteps, Annora placed a finger to her lips.

Three soft taps on the door, and Mrs. Baxter raised the latch and entered.

Mirah, like an ever-present shadow, came in behind her mother, a gloating sneer curling one side of her lips.

"We don't mean to interrupt your visit," the older woman began hesitantly, but something in her demeanor indicated she had news to impart.

"We don't mind," Annora said, deliberately quenching an ominous premonition she had sensed on the pair's arrival. "I've just been admiring these lovely pillow covers. Lesley made them herself." Annora held them up for her guardian to see.

"Why, they're exquisite." Mrs. Baxter beamed at the guest. "You do exceptional stitchery, dear."

"Thank you." A faint blush pinkened Lesley's fair cheeks.

Then the minister's wife returned her attention to Annora. "I thought you might be pleased to know we've set a day for your nuptials."

Annora's mouth went dry, and her fingers clutched a handful of the coverlet beneath her to steady herself. She felt, more than saw, Mirah's satisfied smirk.

"Yes," her guardian went on. "I probably should have waited to announce this tomorrow eve, when young Percival comes to dine with us again. But I just couldn't contain it another moment. Mirah suggested Lesley might like to share in your happy news."

Trembling inwardly, Annora struggled for composure as a sickening dread turned her blood to ice.

"Mistress Fitzpatrick assures me that after tomorrow's final fitting, your trousseau will be delivered the very next day. So we shall schedule the glorious occasion for the week's end. Midafternoon on Saturday." The matron glowed with anticipation.

The triumphant set of Mirah's proud shoulders indicated in eloquent silence her own unbridled glee.

It was all Annora could do to muster a polite smile. She met Lesley's wide blue eyes in wordless misery.

"How exciting!" That her friend's enthusiasm was a sham was obvious to Annora as Lesley grasped her shoulder in a hug. "That is delightful news. I'm so happy for you." But as she leaned close, she put her lips up to Annora's ear. "Remember what I said," she whispered.

"Yes," Mrs. Baxter gushed. "We're thankful the Lord has enabled us to secure such a prosperous union for our Annora."

Lesley cleared her throat and rose to her feet. "Indeed. Well, I'd truly like to stay longer and hear more about the arrangements, but Mother insisted I come directly home. I just had to deliver my bridal gift. Perhaps another time." With a last hug, she gave Annora a pointed stare, then turned with a smile. "I'll be off, then. Good evening, Mrs. Baxter, Mirah."

"Good evening, dear," the minister's wife replied. "I'll show you out." Still smiling from her earlier pronouncement, she nodded to Annora, then ushered the willowy younger woman toward the stairs.

The daughter of the household swung a furtive glance from Annora to Lesley, then back. "I'm just thrilled for you," she gushed in syrupy sweetness. "Positively ecstatic."

You would be, Annora railed silently but held onto her composure as Mirah turned and fairly danced downstairs after the others.

As the sound of their footsteps faded, Annora sank to her knees. . .but the fervent plea of her heart could find no expression. Three days. *Three days*!

❧

Annora slept fitfully and awakened in the chill blue of dawn to hear the ice wagon rumbling up the cobbles on the street below, its vast store of crystal blocks leaving a trail of droplets in its wake. The bearded driver, so tall and lean he appeared to be all bone and gristle, was as regular as morning itself. . .he and the new day both reminders of God's faithfulness.

Her quiet time of prayer and Bible reading also instilled peace within her, and Annora had wrapped her mother's treasures in handkerchiefs and tucked them into the bottom of her drawstring handbag. The moment the opportunity presented itself, she would steal away to Lesley's. With that hope uppermost in her heart, she raced downstairs.

Mrs. Baxter and her daughter were on the bottom landing. "Mirah will be going with you today," the woman informed her.

Annora's spirit drooped low. Detaching herself from the younger girl's overbearing presence would prove difficult now.

The bleak thought only grew stronger as the two of them stood motionless on the dressmaker stools a little over an hour later.

"This is so tiresome!" Mirah fidgeted as the hem was being pinned in her gown. "I can't see why Mother insisted I have a new frock for this silly affair."

Annora could conjure up a few more descriptive terms for the occasion herself but held her tongue and made a quarter turn on her own perch so Gertie could continue around the rich satin skirt of the bridal gown.

"How much longer?" Mirah groused. "My feet hurt. Father should have driven us here in the carriage. And I'm hungry."

"If ye'd be holdin' still, miss," shy, mobcapped Annabelle announced with surprising fervor, "I'd have ye done in two shakes of a lamb's tail."

Mirah folded her arms and huffed but finally relented.

Annora glanced across the workroom at the clock. Almost noon, and not a moment of it without Mirah, whose pouty presence had put a damper on the usual good-natured chatter among the seamstresses. The significant glances passing between them, however, bespoke far more than words. Annora released an unbidden sigh from deep inside.

Just then, the resident cat ambled through the curtained doorway separating the workroom from the main part of the shop. After an elaborate stretch, it sought the soft comfort of its pillowed basket in the corner and curled up with a contented, almost inaudible, purr.

With her back to the animal, Mirah sneezed. "Excuse me," she said, frowning. Then she sneezed again. "I—" Another sneeze followed. "This is just horrid. I don't know what—"

Annora smothered a giggle.

"There." Annabelle rose from her knees. "All done, Miss Baxter."

Mirah all but jumped off the stool and turned to allow the worker to help her off with the gown. She stiffened and her eyes widened. "A cat! No wonder I'm—" A succession of undignified sneezes brought tears. "And I've forgotten to bring a handkerchief." In her camisole and drawers, she scrambled out of the pooled skirts at her ankles and made a dive for Annora's reticule.

Mama's jewelry! Annora's heart all but stopped instantly. "Here, let me help you," she blurted, springing out of Gertie's reach to reclaim her bag from Mirah's fingers.

But the younger girl was already rooting through it. Racked by yet another sneeze, Mirah yanked a lace-trimmed cloth from the bag.

A cameo brooch dropped to the floor between them. Annora cringed and held her breath as Mirah dabbed at her eyes.

"Not to worry, miss," Annabelle said consolingly. "I've whisked Dimples right out of here. He'll not be botherin' ye now."

"The damage has already been done," Mirah said despairingly. She clutched her stomach. "I feel rather ill."

Sliding the brooch out of sight with the toe of her slipper, Annora put an arm about the younger girl. "We need to get you home as quickly as possible."

"The mistress's carriage is out back," Gertie told them. "I'm sure she won't be mindin' if Annabelle borrows it to drive the young miss. Come on, dear. I'll help you dress while Annie checks with Mrs. Fitzpatrick."

Mirah sniffed and nodded and allowed Gertie to lead her away.

Just before they moved behind the dressing screen, Gertie glanced over her shoulder at Annora. "Hope you don't mind stayin' behind. We still have two gowns with hems to mark."

Limp with relief, Annora stooped down and deftly plucked the cameo up and returned it to the safety of her handbag.

Her smile of victory made the whole day brighter.

seven

"Would you tell us a story, Pa?" Amy begged, turning soulful eyes up to Lucas. "Please? Please?"

Her sister's fervent nod gave the request even more weight.

Looking from one sweet face to the other, Lucas was a goner. He straightened from tucking the pair into bed and swiped his shirt sleeve across his forehead. He had so much more to do before dark—but would there ever come a time when that wouldn't be true? Exhaling a weary breath, he cocked one side of his mouth into a smile. "What kind of story?"

"You know, about Baby Moses, like Mama used to tell us."

"No," Melinda corrected. "About the little slave girl who helped her master with lep—lepro— Oh, you know."

"Leprosy. Well, tell you what," Lucas suggested, reluctant to pass on tales he was trying to put out of his mind. "How about I make one up, instead."

"Oh, goody!" Golden-haired Amy sprang to a sitting position and clapped. Then, catching the frown her father leveled at her, she just as quickly lay back down.

He winked, then rubbed his jaw in thought and squatted on one knee beside the bed the little ones shared. "Well, let's see. . ."

"No, Pa. 'Once upon a time,' " Amy said in all seriousness.

"Right. Once upon a time, there was. . .a pony named Star. He was named that because he had this patch of white right about—here." He tapped his youngest daughter's forehead, and she grinned. "Only Star wasn't a very happy little pony."

The two young faces scrunched up.

"Why?" Melinda asked.

"Because he heard his owner tell a stranger that he could

58

buy Star. And Star didn't want to leave his pasture. He was happy there, prancing around with the other ponies. He wanted to stay where he was for a very long time. Maybe forever."

"Ohhh," the girls moaned.

"But what he didn't know," Lucas went on, "was that the strange man had two little girls at his house, who would love Star and take very good care of him."

"So he was really going to a happy place," Melinda chimed in.

"And the little girls would love him lots and lots," Amy added, her blue eyes shining.

"Right." Lucas ruffled their hair, then winced at how stringy it felt. Why were the days so blasted short all the time? He needed extra hours to see to the farm and take care of little ones besides. There was no end to the constant chores.

"Will you buy us a pony someday, Pa?" his older child asked hopefully, cutting into his musings and ending the story.

"I'd love nothing more, pumpkin. . .if the crops sell and the day comes when I can buy that string of good horses I'd like. That won't be for awhile, though."

"It's all right," she said quietly. "Mama told us you always do what you say. . .when the time is right."

Francie had said a lot of things, he recalled. She had set such store by all his grand dreams. But many of those dreams had died with her, and what the girls didn't know was he hardly cared one way or the other about the old plans now. He was just going through the motions. . .and not doing such a good job, judging by the less-than-spotless appearance of these two motherless angels. Their bed sheets didn't look a whole lot better than they did. He rose. "Well, time to sleep now. I'll be right outside, so no whispering."

"But—won't you hear my prayers first?" Melinda asked.

He inhaled slowly. "Sure. Go ahead."

The youngsters steepled their tiny hands and solemnly closed their eyes. "Dear God, thank You for the happy day and the nice story Pa told us. Please give Mama a hug and kiss and tell her we love her. Good night, God. Amen."

"Amen!" Amy echoed.

Lucas had to swallow hard. " 'Night, you two. No whispering, remember." A last smile, and he exited the little room— and promptly tripped over a pile of dirty clothes Melinda had dutifully gathered together.

Man, if that lazy brother of mine deigned to spend half as much time lending a hand around the place as he did gallivanting off to town, maybe the place wouldn't be such a shambles, Lucas groused, picking himself up. He bent to retrieve the soiled laundry to be added to his own stack for wash day tomorrow. He just hoped somebody would soon reply to the notice he'd sent east. And right now, he'd settle for just about *anybody*, no matter how old or decrepit she might turn out to be.

ະ

In a changing room in the church basement, Annora gazed in the full-length looking glass, not even recognizing the person staring back at her. Having stood still as a statue in Mistress Fitzpatrick's Fashion Salon while the exquisite satin bridal gown was pinned and tucked and fitted to perfection, she had never once caught sight of how she actually looked. But here, now, observing the play of light over the folds of rich fabric, the pearls and white sequins shimmering with her slightest movement, her hair in a glorious cluster of ringlets, the enormity of what she was about to do settled oppressively over her spirit.

"I could very nearly cry," Mrs. Baxter said softly, fussing with the fragile veil of tulle and lace, arranging it just so over Annora's red-gold curls. "This is one of the happiest moments of my life." Leaning to bestow a hug, she smiled in the mirror at Annora's reflection. "Pray, do not be nervous. On this most special of all days, you'll be embarking on one of life's wonderful adventures."

"I. . .I don't know how to thank you," Annora said around the thickness in her throat. "You and the Reverend Baxter. You've been very good to me. And I–I'm very—"

"Pshaw!" her guardian exclaimed, obviously taking the incomplete statement as an apology for past wrongs. "All is forgotten. You're going off on your own now. Be happy, that's all we could ask. Now I must go next door and see that Mirah is dressing, then check on a few other details. Nothing to worry yourself over. You've finished so early, you can just relax and think calm thoughts. When everyone has assembled upstairs in the sanctuary, and we're ready for you, I'll send Mirah."

"Thank you." Unable to meet the older woman's gaze, Annora smiled thinly and pretended to be entranced by her own reflected image. And all the while she listened to her guardian's diminishing footsteps, her pulse throbbed with increasing intensity.

At last the door at the top of the stairs clicked shut. Reminding herself to breathe, Annora waited a full two minutes, then crept up the steps, straining to listen for an indication of anyone else's presence in the building. Hearing none, she let herself out the side door.

Then she grasped her skirts and ran for all she was worth.

≈

The Southern and Western Railroad Station in Philadelphia occupied a significant portion of South Broad Street. Annora tamped down her nervousness as she, Lesley, and Lesley's beau, Michael Porter, joined the noisy throng of eager, excited people surging into the great arched hall. Once inside the vast interior, all sounds magnified accordingly, competing with the hisses and bursts of steam from the waiting locomotives, the chugging coughs of the departing ones. Annora eyed the flaring stacks with alarm, already having second thoughts about her impetuous act.

"Are you positive you've got everything?" Lesley asked, straightening the collar of the apple green linen traveling suit she had loaned Annora. "Michael has already seen to your luggage, and I've packed a feast for you in the basket." At Annora's bleak look, she gave her a reassuring hug.

"You're doing the right thing," the brown-eyed young man said confidently, clamping her shoulder. "It will all work out in the end, you'll see."

"Yes. Do stop worrying," Lesley gently scolded her. "You look divine."

"Then why do I feel like a louse?" Annora asked miserably. "You should have seen Mrs. Baxter's face, Les. She almost *loved* me."

"Yes. Almost. That about says it. What she loved most was this chance to pass you off to the first available taker."

"Perhaps." Annora swallowed. "Well, I don't know how I'll repay you both for all your help. I'll never forget it."

"I should hope not." Even though said in a teasing tone, Lesley quickly blinked away sudden moisture in her eyes. "You must promise to write the very minute you get settled. So *I* can stop worrying. You hear?"

Nodding and fighting her own tears, Annora tried to smile.

"All abo—arrr—d," a deep voice called above the hubbub.

Annora's feet refused to move until her friends propelled her from behind. Nearing the portable steps to the huge passenger car, she felt herself being swamped with hugs.

"Take care, Nora. God be with you," Lesley breathed.

The sight of her friends' faces blurred behind a sheen of tears, and Annora could not speak. She touched her fingers to her lips and pressed them to Lesley's, braved as much smile as she could to Michael, and mounted the steps. Turning on the landing, she lifted a hand in final farewell, then before her last shred of composure dissolved, she stumbled, unseeing, into the paneled car.

❧

Someone gently nudged Annora's shoulder.

"Ticket, miss."

Opening her swollen eyes and lifting her head from where it rested against the sooty window, she beheld the portly conductor, resplendent in his crisp navy blue uniform. "I–I must have dozed off," she responded inanely. Exhausted from the sleepless nights leading up to her almost-wedding, the steady rhythm of the steel rails had lulled her into oblivion. Her head throbbed as she rummaged through her reticule and placed her ticket in his extended hand.

A quick perusal, and he punched it with a small silver tool, then returned it to her and continued up the aisle.

Annora averted her gaze, chagrined that strangers might have been staring at her as she slept—a possibility she found less than comforting. But many of the remaining seats were unoccupied, and of the handful of passengers ahead, no one seemed to be paying her any mind. She exhaled slowly and relaxed a bit as the gently swaying car clacked along the rails.

"Well, I see you've returned to the land of the living," a woman's voice said from nearby.

Turning, Annora met the face of an elegantly attired young woman across the aisle and one row back. With dark hair and olive skin, she appeared only a few years older than Annora and held a small babe in her arms. Annora remembered having caught a brief glimpse of the woman through the blur of tears as she'd made her way to her own seat some hours ago.

"I hope I didn't make any embarrassing sounds," Annora said, feeling the warmth of a blush. She noted the classic beauty of the mother's face, framed as it was by its fashionable bonnet, and suspected her own appearance must surely show the effects of anxiety and the sad Philadelphia parting. Unconsciously, she reached up to touch her bonnet.

The woman smiled kindly. "Not at all. I was only concerned that you might awaken with a stiff neck. I'm afraid these seats aren't conducive to restful sleep. I'm Hope Johnston."

"Annora Nolan. Pleased to meet you." Her gaze dropped to the child. "How old is your baby?"

"Four months, already, and growing like a veritable weed. The time flies so quickly." She paused. "I. . .couldn't help noticing you're alone. Are you journeying far?" the narrow-shouldered mother asked.

"Quite far. Wyoming, actually. Cheyenne."

"Why, what a splendid coincidence! Little Rachel and I are on our way to join my husband at Fort Russell! We'll practically be neighbors—for out west, anyway. I was afraid there wouldn't be a living soul with whom to pass the long, dreary journey we have ahead of us. . .that is, if you don't mind listening to a chatterbox. I do tend to get carried away—or so I've been told."

Drawing indescribable comfort from the very concept, Annora grinned. "I think that is what I need the most just now." She gathered her basket and handbag and moved to the empty seat just behind the one she now occupied to make conversation easier. "Chatter away."

By the time the western sky was displaying bands of deepening colors, Annora had acquired a new friend. *How like the Lord*, she decided, *to send along one of His angels—and a knowledgeable one at that.* She took it as a sign of God's approval.

After having come east for the birth of her first child, Hope was now leaving her parents' home in the Philadelphia suburb of Doylestown and making the return trip to her husband's side. She had not only made the westward journey once before, but she knew the intricacies of changing from one train to the next all along the route. Annora breathed a prayer of humble thankfulness, and the greatest sense of peace she had known in a very long time flowed through her being. It made the poignant memory of the bosom friend she'd left behind a little less sad.

Her trepidation at what lay ahead never quite left her, however. What if this Lucas Brent had already hired another housekeeper? What would she do then?

eight

The hiss of steam and the clanging bell were deafening as Annora finally stepped off the train in Wyoming several endless days later. She moved as far from the noise as possible, staying out of the way of the clusters of people greeting arriving individuals or bidding farewell to those about to depart.

Her head buzzed with the information Hope Johnston had passed on regarding the territory in general and Cheyenne in particular. But despite all the preparation, Annora's heart plummeted when she took her first actual look at the bustling frontier town.

It was even worse than her imaginings. No cobbled, tree-lined streets here nor tidy rows of impressive business establishments. No huge river upon whose tides ocean vessels came and went. Instead, wooden sidewalks teemed with vagabond strollers, savage-looking miners, high-booted and shaggy-haired roughs, scouts in buckskins, young men wearing military blue, and rambunctious children. And there was no lack of saloons or gaming places. The loud ruckus spilling out of some buildings in the vicinity made that very obvious, as did the appearance of some rather scraggly-looking individuals loitering near them.

As Annora waited on the wide, level platform for her luggage to be unloaded, the hot afternoon wind whipped a sheet of dust over her. She brushed futilely at her already sooty and wrinkled traveling suit. Some grand impression she would make if Mr. Brent lived in town. . .and if he didn't, that presented problems of a whole different nature.

"There you go, Miss Nolan," a railroad man said, setting her trunk down next to the valise she had kept with her.

She smiled her thanks, wondering if there could possibly be a single article of clothing inside her luggage that would be less wrinkled than what she had on. During her final three days in Philadelphia, she had sneaked all the clothing she could manage over to Lesley's, and her friend had taken over, packing as much as would fit into an old trunk in her parents' attic. Annora wasn't even sure what all she had with her, and the best she'd been able to do during the journey was sponge her face and hands clean from time to time and brush as much soot from her ensemble as possible.

"Well, Annora," Hope said, approaching her from behind, "I wish you every happiness in your new venture."

Annora turned to step into a parting hug that included the two of them and tiny Rachel as well. "Thank you. I was so glad to find a friend on that tiresome trip, Hope. I'm convinced the Lord put you there just for me."

Easing away, the brunette smiled, cuddling her sleeping baby daughter closer. "Actually, I thought it was the other way around. But in any case, I, too, am glad to know I have a friend in Cheyenne. Our paths may cross again one of these days."

"Now, wouldn't that be a treat!"

"Indeed. Well, I must go and check to see what the departure time is for the stage to the fort. I'll be keeping you in my prayers."

"And I, you. Take care of that sweet little angel." Watching her new friend walk away, Annora felt greatly comforted just knowing that at least one familiar face lived in this wild, unknown territory. But she wasn't completely at ease after Hope strolled off. She was all on her own, now—and hadn't the slightest idea where to go.

Well, she affirmed silently, *I can start with the clerk at the ticket window.* "Excuse me, sir," she said, nearing him.

The short, small-featured man standing inside the cutout window of the station peered at her between the brim of his visor and a pair of spectacles perched halfway down his nose.

"I was wondering if you might be able to tell me where Mr. Lucas Brent lives or how I might contact him."

"Brent," he repeated, squinting his eyes in thought. "His place is half a dozen miles or so outside of town. But—" he pointed to someone loading a pair of barrels onto a wagon— "I reckon that young fellow over yonder should be able to take you right to the man's door. That's where he's goin'."

"Splendid!" Annora exclaimed, wondering over yet another miracle. Her parents had instilled in her long ago the fact that God cares for His own, and she was finding that to be very true. Had He arranged for this individual to be here at the very moment she needed transportation? She dared not consider what she'd do if he happened to refuse. Hope had reported that people in the territory were quite helpful and friendly, especially to newcomers, common as they were. Praying that was the case, Annora made her way to the young man's rig, glancing over his muscular frame and sable hair as she got closer. "I beg your pardon?"

Blue eyes glanced in her direction as he straightened. "Talking to me, miss?"

"Yes. I–I'm trying to get to Mr. Lucas Brent's place. Do you know where it is?" She nibbled her lip hopefully.

He eyed her boldly, a smile twitching a corner of his mouth. "Matter of fact, I do. You have business with him?"

"Yes. Well, no. That is. . .I'm hoping the position he advertised is still open. I've come to apply for it. I wrote him a letter—" Afraid to confess it had been barely two weeks past, Annora cut the explanation short. "I'd be willing to pay for a ride, if you see fit to take me there."

"You don't say." A spark of humor shone in his eyes as he appeared to consider the request, and for some reason it prickled Annora. "Have any luggage?"

"One trunk, plus a small valise."

"That's it?"

She nodded.

"Well, point me to them, miss. Looks like I'm your man."

Within moments, she found herself aboard the wagon seat, her baggage loaded into the bed of the rig. From this perspective she had an opportunity to get a closer look at the town she expected would be her new home.

Cheyenne did offer some respectability—at least for a span of two or three blocks—with neat brick buildings, an attractive show of shop windows, and even a three-story hotel. But beyond that it relapsed into a bold disregard of architectural style. Almost every ten paces along the dusty streets sat a saloon or barroom offering games of chance.

Annora was greatly relieved to count a few churches and a decent schoolhouse in passing as the driver guided the team out of town, heading westward. "I'm Annora Nolan," she finally remembered to say, her voice wavering as the wheels lurched over the uneven ruts.

"Just call me Noah."

"That would be somewhat forward, I dare say."

He shrugged. "Not in these parts, it ain't."

Not entirely certain he wasn't toying with her, Annora felt a little ill at ease and shifted on the seat. But the smile he turned on her didn't seem particularly threatening, only—peculiar. She tried to relax, taking in the openness of the landscape in comparison to Pennsylvania's thickly forested hills. A liberal sprinkling of sagebrush and other strange-looking scrubby bushes dotted the parched grassland for miles. "Do you know Mr. Brent personally?" she asked after a short silence.

"You might say that."

"Oh, I suppose everyone knows everyone else around here."

He merely grinned.

Really! Annora thought. *I'm simply trying to make polite conversation.* Releasing a small sigh, she crossed her ankles and hands and straightened her spine. She directed her attention to the scenery again, wondering exactly how much farther it was to Mr. Brent's.

After an interminable amount of time, the wagon pulled off the main road and onto a lane. Once they had crested a small knoll, a group of farm buildings came into view. There was a rather dismal frame house with a porch across its front, a fairly large barn, and several outbuildings.

A wide section of land beyond had been plowed and planted with what appeared to have been corn, recently harvested. The leftover shocks had been cut and stacked about the field. Rows of other crops were also visible. The varied greens contrasted sharply to the surrounding arid land. "Is–is that—"

"Yep."

Annora waited for additional information, but none followed. She tamped down nervous flutterings in the pit of her stomach, wishing she had thought to prepare a speech during the oppressively silent drive from town. Only a few moments now remained to come up with one. She frowned in concentration. *Good day, Mr. Brent. I've come in answer to your notice*. At that inadequate try, she cringed. *Why, it's a pleasure to meet you, Mr. Brent. I do hope you received my letter*. She rolled her eyes, finally settling on a frantic silent prayer instead.

The petition was interrupted by girlish squeals. "Noah! Noah's coming!"

Annora followed the sound of the voices to two little urchins jumping up and down on the porch. And the nearer the rig drew to the place, the greater Annora's disquiet. The poor things were so thin. Thin and filthy, their little dresses soiled and torn.

As the children spied her, they turned silent and stood still, the older one sliding an arm around the younger. Even as the assurance flowed through Annora that the position must still be open, doubts about her foolhardiness drained it away. Perhaps Mr. Brent was riffraff, the ungodly sort, impossible to work for. He might have even driven three or four applicants away already. And who knows what his temperament would be like? Her hands began to tremble.

Noah stopped the wagon near the edge of the yard and hopped down. Still staring at the unkempt children, Annora suddenly realized he was waiting to assist her. She gathered her courage and stood, then leaned into his upraised hands.

He set her on her feet. Then without a word, he went to unload her things before climbing aboard the rig and driving it toward the barn, whistling as he went.

Assuming that was where the goods from town needed to go, Annora smiled at the girls, who scarcely moved a muscle as they stared mutely at her. She shifted from one foot to the other, keenly aware that in all likelihood, she didn't look so good herself. "I've come to see your father," she finally said in what she hoped was a pleasant tone. "Is he here?"

The two exchanged wary glances, then the older one nodded.

"Would you please go and get him for me?"

After a split-second's hesitation, the pair took one another's hands and jumped off the porch, running past the barn.

૨ⴰ

"Pa! Pa!"

Discerning an unusual note of alarm in his older daughter's voice, Lucas paused in replacing the chicken wire and turned so he could scoop the two children up in his arms the minute they reached him. He'd heard the wagon rumbling over the lane and concluded that Noah must have finally arrived with the supplies. But what could be upsetting the girls?

Melinda got to him first, and he wrapped one arm around her and the other around Amy, a step behind. "It's a lady, Pa. Come to see you."

A lady? The only one of those he knew was Rosemary, and the youngsters would surely recognize her. He scratched the few days' growth of stubble on his face. *Must be someone else from town.* With a shrug and a cheery grin at his daughters, he took each by the hand and allowed them to lead him to the house, wishing he could clean up a bit for *company*.

Coming within sight of the visitor waiting just shy of the porch, he stopped short. She was turned away slightly, her petite form as slim as a quill. Lucas had no idea what someone so young could want with him. Especially someone whose appearance was that of one who'd been traveling for a long time. He squeezed his daughters' hands and smiled down at them. "How about checking for any new eggs while I tend to the *lady?*"

"Yes, Pa." They skipped happily off, and Lucas continued up the path to the yard.

She swung to look at him as he approached.

Lucas had never seen eyes such a light green before—or did they just seem so?—set above fine, high cheekbones in that guileless face and crowned with slender tapered brows. He gave himself a mental shake. "My daughters said you were asking for me? I'm Lucas Brent. What can I do for you, miss?"

A tentative smile curved her rosy lips at the edges, and she extended a gloved hand. "Pleased to make your acquaintance. I'm Annora Nolan."

She'd said it like an announcement, but her name meant absolutely nothing to Lucas. He maintained a blank stare and watched her confidence fall a few notches.

"I–I wrote you a letter. Hasn't it arrived yet?"

"You mean—"

"Yes!" she gasped in relief, obviously assuming he knew what she was talking about. "I've come to apply for the position you advertised."

With a quick glance that took her in from head to toe, Lucas fought the urge to laugh in derision. A fragile, refined gal like her wasn't even old enough to have developed any of the qualifications a more mature woman would have arrived with. She was no more a housekeeper than he was a sawbones! And worse yet, even with that red hair of hers twisted into the semblance of a knot beneath that prim bonnet, she was hardly more than a baby herself! He needed help, sure—but this little filly would be just one more little girl to look after! The whole idea was absurd. He opened his mouth to tell her just that.

Noah chose just that moment to stroll up from the barn. "See you've met our new housekeeper," he said, grinning like a barn cat by a pail of spilled milk.

Lucas branded his kid brother with a sizzling glare. "And just what part did you play in this?"

Shoulders and brows rose as one in supreme innocence. "She asked me to drive her here. That's as much as I know."

Returning his attention to the visitor, Lucas saw shock tinged with mortification paint two rosy circles on her fair cheeks. Lips pressed into a thin line, she gaped from Noah to him, then back, looking from all appearances as if she was on the verge of bolting and running the whole seven miles back to town.

He held up a calming hand. "All right. Let's stop this whole thing here and now. I need to get a few little details straight. First of all, Miss—Nolan, did you say?"

She nodded, a frown still crinkling her brows.

"I take it you've met my brother, Noah."

Her eyes hardened. "He only gave his first name. I assumed he was a delivery man."

Noah averted his gaze and tried to appear guiltless, even with his tongue teasing his cheek.

"Figures," Lucas grated in disgust. He switched back to the redhead. "And you say you wrote me a letter."

She swallowed. "Yes. From Philadelphia. I saw your notice on the public board at my church and applied for the position some weeks ago."

Noah drew a crumpled blue-gray envelope from the inside pocket of his vest. "Postmaster gave this to me today. Says he found it wedged between the wall and his desk. Didn't know how long it'd been there."

At the sight of the stationery she had found in Mrs. Baxter's old lap desk, Annora realized he had never even gotten it! She wanted to crawl into the nearest hole. And die.

Lucas kneaded his jaw. Reaching for the missive, he opened it and scanned through the single page she had written. Then he released a whoosh of breath. He'd been stupid enough to think every unimaginable thing that could possibly happen to a man had already come his way. But now this!

He turned to his brother. "Hitch the wagon back up," he ordered sternly, avoiding the girl's widening green eyes. "Miss Nolan needs a ride to town."

nine

"No!" Realizing she had actually stomped her foot, Annora felt her face turn a vivid shade of crimson as Noah halted in his tracks and turned.

Both men's astonished blue eyes leveled straight on her.

Annora centered on the most penetrating ones, those in dark-haired Lucas Brent's unsmiling face, and spoke much more softly to regain her composure. "I can't go back. Please, don't send me away."

The brothers swapped incredulous glances, and the elder of the two shook his head. "Look, miss, I'm sure you meant well by taking it upon yourself to come here unannounced—"

"I sent a letter," Annora reiterated slowly, distinctly.

He turned his gaze skyward and shrugged, palms up.

Annora had no choice but to plead her case. "The notice said 'In desperate need.' Has that changed? Has anyone else come to help out? Or even offered?"

"No," Mr. Brent admitted.

"Then, give me a chance. That's all I ask. I've come all this way, and—"

"She's right." Noah, who had only watched the exchange up until this point, finally spoke up.

The farmer cut him a glower. "Don't be ridiculous." Switching his attention to Annora once more, he shifted his stance and raised a calloused hand as if he was about to shake a finger in her face. But with an exasperated huff, he lowered his arm instead. "Miss Nolan."

She bristled at his placating tone.

"I appreciate your generous offer," he went on. "I really do. But as you can see, I already have two little girls to look after.

I do not—I repeat, *not*—need a third. If you really want to help me out, go back home. I'm sure your parents are worried about you."

Annora hiked her chin. "My parents are dead. I have no home."

"About figures," he mumbled under his breath.

Spying the children heading toward them, the egg basket looped over the older one's arm, Annora moved a little farther out on the limb. "And it appears to me your daughters could stand a little more 'looking after.' "

Noah snickered.

Lucas Brent's head drooped, and he rubbed at his temples. He did not say a word.

"A month." Annora urged in her most businesslike manner. "Give me a month's trial. Let me prove I can cook, clean, and care for your daughters. Then if you feel I'm not doing a good job, or if another woman comes along whom you feel is better qualified, you. . .you can ask me to leave."

"Sounds fair enough," Noah piped in.

His older brother opened his mouth to reply, but one of the children sidled up to him, shyly taking stock of the stranger. "I'm hungry, Pa. When's supper?"

Annora thought she discerned an easing of the man's determination, a slight resignation in the sag of one broad shoulder. He gazed down at his girls, then up at her. "You say you can cook?"

"That's right."

"Well, then, there's the house. Let's see what you can do." He turned on his heel and strode back in the direction from which he'd come.

A fraction of Annora's fear subsided. He was giving her a chance!

"Whoo-eee!" Noah smacked one knee with his open palm and sauntered to the barn.

The girls, peering hesitantly after both of them, lifted their dirty faces to Annora. "What's your name, lady?"

❧

Annora's spirit had hit rock bottom at her first disheartening glimpse of the chaos greeting her inside the dwelling. But after unearthing some dried fruit for the girls to nibble on while they went back outside to play, she slipped off the jacket of Lesley's once-spotless suit, rolled up her sleeves, and filled a big kettle with water to heat on the cookstove. She turned and faced the disaster behind her and took a deep breath. She would set the living quarters to rights or die trying. . .and for the first time ever, she thanked her Heavenly Father for all those months she'd been forced into drudgery at the Baxters'.

Melinda and Amy had shown her to the smokehouse, so Annora put some meat on to stew while she labored with broom, scrub brush, and dust cloth. Before long the hidden charm of the little house began to make its appearance. Annora tried to envision a young wife and mother bustling about, tidying up, rubbing oil into the mantel, shining the glass chimneys of the lamps. . .typical duties that maintained a proper home. And there were a few inexpensive pieces of bric-a-brac and framed embroidered samplers on the walls, niceties that a woman takes pleasure in displaying. She wondered what sort of woman the late mistress of the house had been.

Then Annora's thoughts drifted to the tall, lean-faced man who at present was her employer. She estimated he was at least ten years her senior. His bluish-gray eyes were shaded by straight brows the identical black-brown of his hair. . .and held more than a trace of sadness. But it wasn't hard to imagine that tanned face without its set jaw, without the creases the obvious intense pain of bereavement had wrought.

In fact, she decided, he could actually be considered quite. . . handsome, under all that stubble. She had caught tiny glimpses of his softer side when he looked at his daughters. Surely even someone as gruff as he could not be all bad. But considering how intimidated she had felt in his presence, Annora blushed at the shameless way she had stood up to him. She had even surprised herself, if the truth were told—but she chalked it up to desperation bringing previously unknown qualities to the fore.

Chopping fresh vegetables and adding them to the stew, she inhaled the rich broth simmering on the stove and concluded it would turn out as tasty as Mrs. Henderson's. The woman had been a wonderful teacher. Now, to stir up some biscuits.

It was dusk by the time Annora finished the living room and kitchen. Way past the normal supper hour. But stepping out onto the porch to ring the dinner bell, she knew it could have been much worse. She willed aside the aching of her entire body and clanged the iron rod against the triangle, fighting an impulse to laugh as a veritable stampede of feet followed immediately.

"Hey, you two. Wash up for supper," Lucas ordered, snagging his little girls midstep in their mad dash to the porch. He steered them to the rain barrel and dipped a liberal amount into the basin on the stand beside it. While they soaped their hands, he took a towel and scrubbed the childish faces. Then they scampered off. He splashed some of the cold liquid over his face and neck, dried off, and followed the tantalizing and almost forgotten smell of good cooking into his house.

He could not believe his eyes. For the first time since Francie's passing, the place—at least what he could see of it from the doorway—was clean and orderly. The table sported a fresh tablecloth, something he never bothered with. And Miss Nolan had even cut some roses from the scraggly bush outside for the middle of the table.

"These are my mama's Sunday dishes," Melinda said accusingly, as she and her sister climbed onto their chairs. "We're not supposed to use the Sunday dishes unless there's company."

"Company," Amy echoed with a decided nod.

Carrying a serving bowl of stew over from the sideboard, Annora Nolan blanched, making the sprinkling of freckles across the bridge of her pert nose more distinct.

Lucas knew only a blind man would fail to see how spent the young woman was when she set the burden down. A twinge of remorse shot through him at the thought of how he'd taken advantage of her. . .dumping the whole sorry mess on those slender shoulders, and after that exhausting journey, yet! He ruffled his older daughter's hair. "It's all right, pumpkin. Miss Nolan *is* company tonight."

The explanation seemed to satisfy the girls.

Noah clomped across the porch and entered then, his face aglow from a vigorous washing. A grin broadened his boyish features, sending a twinkle to his eyes as he pulled out a chair and sat down. "I'd say you've got yourself a job, little lady. I won't need to be traipsin' off to town to get a decent meal anymore, with you around."

She almost smiled as she set a plate of hot biscuits next to the stew, then turned away.

"Aren't you eating?" Lucas asked with a frown.

"I'll wait until the family is finished," she said, casting her gaze to the floor. "I'm only the housekeeper."

"Hmph. That might be the way things are done back East," he replied. "But out here, folks eat together. Set yourself a place."

"Yes, sir."

"And don't call me sir."

She caught her bottom lip in her teeth and did as told. After easing to her seat, she bowed her head.

Lucas stared for a second or two, and warmth climbed his neck. He cleared his throat. "We quit wasting time on grace here. . .but if you're set on it, we won't stop you." He lowered his head but did not close his eyes.

"Dear Heavenly Father," she began, "thank You for bringing

me safely to Wyoming. We thank You for these provisions and ask Your blessing on them. And thank You that Mr. Brent has given me this chance. Please help me do my best for him. I ask these things in Your Son's name. Amen."

An uncomfortable knot formed in Lucas's throat. The simple way she talked to the Almighty brought a remembrance of Francie's intimate friendship with God—one he had shared—and another wave of guilt washed over him. He couldn't even remember the last time he had prayed. Collecting his thoughts, he ladled stew into his daughters' bowls and took some himself, savoring every mouthful as he ate. . .but never once meeting those arresting green eyes farther down the table.

"Mmm. This is real good," Amy proclaimed.

Melinda, downing her entire glass of milk in a quick succession of gulps, only nodded.

Noah, occupying the foot of the table, was already helping himself to seconds. "Best I've had in a dog's age," he said with a broad grin and reached for a couple more biscuits.

The delicious meal was already more than Lucas would have expected. But the warm apple pandowdy topped with rich cream earned applause from the little ones. He had to admit, it went perfectly with the fresh coffee in his mug.

Noting absently that there seemed a bit less conversation during dessert, Lucas chalked it up to the lateness of the hour, or the fact that everyone had been so hungry to start with. But suddenly even the girls stopped chattering. Looking up, he saw their attention was centered on Miss Nolan, sitting straight as a poker, her hands folded in her lap. . .sound asleep.

"Would you look at that," Noah murmured. "She's plumb wore out."

Feeling a new onslaught of reproach, Lucas quietly eased his chair back and got up, skirting the table. He swept the new housekeeper up into his arms and carried her to his bedroom, where he laid her gently on the bed and flicked a light blanket over her sleeping form.

The glow of the lamplight from the other room illuminated that classic, heart-shaped face of hers, now as innocent and trusting as a child's. Lucas caught himself staring, then shook his head and left the room, closing the door behind him without a sound.

Annora. He mulled it over in his mind. *Suits her.* She'd weighed less than a feather in his arms.

Then, before he let himself get caught up in thoughts he didn't need to be having, he strode purposely to the kitchen. The least he could do was get the dishes out of the way and dunk the girls in the tub. It would give the little gal from Philadelphia a bit less to wake up to.

But he couldn't help smiling at the remembered sight of the fiery young redhead asleep at the table.

ten

Annora sensed someone's presence as she slowly came to consciousness. She raised her lashes to find two sets of solemn blue eyes studying her.

The children were leaning over on the bed, elbows resting on it, chins cupped in their hands.

"She's waking up," Amy whispered.

Her big sister nudged her. "She's already awake, silly. See?"

With sudden awareness, Annora flew to a sitting position. It was morning! She was in someone's bed! Worse yet, she had no idea how she had gotten there. Even in her muddled state she absorbed the room's simple furnishings. . .a plain double bed, a washstand, and an armoire. Her trunk and valise had been set on the floor against one wall. But how had she come to be here?

"This is our mama's bed," Melinda announced.

"Pa had to sleep outside," the little one added.

"In the barn."

Trying to process that humiliating information, Annora went back in her mind over the previous evening. The last she could recall, she had just served dessert and was listening to the pleasant chatter between the young sisters about a special new litter of barn kittens. There was a tiny fragment of a dream, however, of being held in someone's arms. . . She swallowed. "I–I must make breakfast!"

"Huh-uh," they chorused, heads wagging slowly back and forth.

"You've already eaten?

They nodded.

Annora's heart sank. The very first day in this household,

trying to prove she could take care of all the necessary duties, and she'd overslept! Disgusted with herself, she cast her gaze toward the ceiling, then swung her legs over the side of the mattress and stood. "Well, then, I'll have to find something else to do, won't I?" She smiled at the urchins, noticing that even though they were wearing the same clothes as yesterday, they themselves appeared cleaner.

"You prob'ly have to go to the privy," Melinda informed her in six-year-old importance.

"You can use the pot under the bed," Amy suggested.

Despite her disquiet, Annora barely stifled a giggle. She was going to like these two. Looking from one to the other, she affirmed their opposite coloring, something she had noticed only subconsciously in the busyness of yesterday. Melinda, the older one, had her father's olive complexion and brunette hair, whereas four-year-old Amy was fair and golden blond. But they were equally engaging. She smiled at them both, then focused on Melinda. "After I've been to the privy, I'll need to find the washtub and soap so I can start on the laundry."

"Come on. I'll show you." The dark-haired youngster slid a small hand into Annora's and began leading her toward the kitchen door. "Pa already filled the big kettle. It's on the stove."

Chagrined, Annora had to be thankful that she wouldn't be wasting still more of this morning waiting for the water to heat. But how would she ever face Mr. Brent after this blunder? As it was, the very sight of those blue eyes of his sent feelings through her that she had never before experienced. And something about his presence made her knees feel a little weak. But whatever low opinion he must surely have of her now, she would, at the very least, see to it that he and his brother had a decent dinner, come noon.

Thanks to the helpful little guides, Annora soon found herself up to her elbows in sudsy water. Within a couple hours, the two long clotheslines were filled with newly washed items billowing in the ever-present breeze. The sight was gratifying, as was the amazing speed at which they dried. She even felt better herself, having freshened up in the privacy of the bedroom and changed into a navy cotton skirt and plain white shirtwaist.

Returning to the kitchen, she raised the towel covering the rising bread to check its progress, then smiled. The loaves would be done for supper. Right now, everyone would have to settle for more biscuits. She gave the big pot of beans and bacon a stir, then removed a double batch of golden biscuits from the oven. With a quick glance at the table, she smiled her approval and went to ring the bell.

ze

Lucas wiped his mouth on the cloth napkin and got up, shoving the chair away with the backs of his knees. "That was one fine meal, Miss Nolan. Thank you."

"I'm glad you enjoyed it," she said softly.

"That's puttin' it mildly," Noah declared. "I was starved without even knowin' it!" Snatching one more biscuit from the diminished stack, he pocketed it in his jeans and gave a satisfied nod as he headed outside.

Noting that his brother had spent the better portion of the meal gawking at *the help*, Lucas quickly followed after him. He'd better remind the kid that this arrangement was only temporary.

"Mr. Brent?"

One foot already over the threshold, Lucas paused and turned, a hand braced on the doorjamb.

"I–I must apologize," Annora stammered. "About last night, I mean. Falling asleep, and all."

"Happens to the best of us, one time or another," he said gently. Unable to put out of his mind how young and vulnerable she had appeared when he'd placed her on the bed, he had purposely refrained from looking directly at her during the meal. Now, however, he could no longer avoid it.

In everyday clothes, her hair brushed and pinned in an

intricate coil at the nape of her neck, she seemed more delicate than ever. And who could miss the way the waistband of
Francie's long apron met in the middle of her back, with the
ties dangling almost to her ankles? She seemed like a little
girl playing at being grown up.

All the more reason not to saddle her with the endless
chores running this house entailed. He really wanted someone
older. Someone. . .substantial. But he'd as much as agreed to
this trial, so no sense putting a damper on things. She was trying real hard to please. . .and this would only be for a couple
weeks. What could happen? He winced. Better have that talk
with Noah. Today.

≈

Once the dishes had been taken care of and the kitchen
restored to order, Annora retrieved a bar of rose-scented soap
from her valise and took the remains of the heated water in
the kettle outside near the rain barrel. She knew the men were
occupied, and this was a perfect opportunity to tend to
another desperately needed chore.

"What 'cha doin'?"

Annora smiled at the girls as they gravitated to her from the
porch step, where they'd been standing all the extra clothes-
pins in a row. "I need to wash my hair."

"In the daytime?" Melinda's tone indicated the concept was
completely unheard of.

"Well, I got kind of dirty on my long train ride, and this is
the first chance I've had to wash some of that off."

"Oh."

Unpinning her chignon, Annora bent over at the waist and
poured warm water over her head. Even just that felt wonderful. She had never before gone an extended period without
having a chance to bathe properly. Application of the soap
made leftover soot from the tiring journey feel like grit under
her fingertips, but at least it was coming out.

"Mama had long hair like yours," Amy said wistfully.

"Only it wasn't red," Melinda supplied. "It was blond like Amy's."

"You must miss her a lot." Reaching for the pitcher again, Annora dipped it into the rain barrel, then squeezed her eyes closed as she rinsed with the cool, clean water.

"Why did God take our mama away?" Melinda asked.

The poignant question tore at Annora's heart. She knew exactly how the little ones felt. Wrapping her hair in one of the clean towels, she flipped it behind her back and stooped down to their level. "I'm afraid only God knows that for sure, sweetheart."

"Miss Rosemary, in town, says God needed Mama to help Him in Heaven. But we need her, too."

Annora wondered who Rosemary was and what her relationship to this little family might be, then decided that the matter would probably become clear during the month ahead. Turning her attention to the children again, she gathered them close. "Well, whatever the Lord's reasons for taking her, that doesn't mean He doesn't still love you. Your mama still loves you, too, and she'll always be with you in your heart. She probably asked God to send extra angels to watch over you, since she can't do it herself."

"Do you think so?"

"Mm-hm. Know what else?"

"What?"

"My mommy and daddy live up there, too. I'll wager they were real happy to have your mama for their new neighbor. They've probably been showing her all around those golden streets and introducing her to Ruth and Jonah and the apostle Paul."

Amy's azure eyes grew soft as she appeared to ponder the thought. Then she brightened. "Wanna come see the new baby kitties in the barn?"

"Their eyes aren't open yet," Melinda added. "They're so cute."

"I'd really like that—if you'll help me for a little while in the garden afterward."

The pair traded glances and nodded.

❧

Grooming Chesapeake in the end stall, Lucas heard the patter of skipping feet approaching. He glanced up at the cheerful threesome—his two little ones and a gal who could easily pass for their older sister. Especially with that red-gold hair of hers loose and splayed over her shoulders. It didn't seem fair for someone so fragile as she to have so much responsibility laid on her all at once. Obviously she was an efficient worker, but he couldn't get past the conviction that she should still be at home, helping her own mother or aunt or other relative. Even having some fun.

He wasn't purposely trying to hide his presence, but as they clustered around the box of sleeping kittens, they were obviously unaware that he was there. Muted oohs drifted to his ears as they fawned over the tiny creatures. Not wanting to intrude, Lucas kept stroking the brush over the sorrel back.

"Pa says we can't pick them up yet," Melinda said.

Amy nodded. "It makes Wilhelmina nervous."

Miss Nolan had an arm on each of the girls' shoulders, and she drew them a little closer to herself. "Well, thank you for showing me your special kitties. Wilhelmina doesn't know who I am yet, though, so I'd better get back to work now."

"Didn't you say we could help?" Melinda asked.

"If you want to."

Watching after them as they exited the barn, Lucas reminded himself to concentrate on what he was doing. But the animal's reddish hide reminded him of Annora Nolan's shiny hair. Stifling any further thoughts, he patted the stallion's muscled neck and put down the brush. This was as good a time as any to talk to Noah.

He found his brother just outside, lounging against the fence, still grasping the hoe he was returning to the shed.

"She's some looker, ain't she?" Noah remarked. "Can't be more'n two or three years younger than me, either. Maybe I'll—"

"No, you won't. She's here for that month she talked her way into. No more. You leave her be."

A corner of Noah's mouth rose sardonically. "What I do is my business."

"As long as you're on my place, it's not." Lucas wrapped his fingers around the handle of Noah's hoe, his gaze unrelenting in a silent challenge.

"We'll have to see about that, won't we?" With a snide grimace, the kid jerked the tool free and stalked off toward the shed.

Lucas released a pent-up breath. Maybe he should rethink this whole matter of her staying, before things got too sticky.

☙

Annora picked up on a subtle tension between the brothers that evening as they ate their ham slices and mashed potatoes in stony silence. Feeling the outsider, she pretended not to notice and did her best to respond to the girls' remarks whenever necessary. But she was relieved when dessert was over and everyone started to go their separate ways.

She snagged her employer again as he was about to leave the house. "Mr. Brent?"

He glanced over his shoulder, then turned to face her.

"I've been thinking," she began. "About the sleeping arrangements."

"We'll just keep them as they are, for now."

"But that's not necessary, really. I shouldn't be putting you out of your own bed. Your daughters need you to be near if they wake up in the middle of the night."

"So what are you suggesting? The barn, maybe? Noah sleeps in the loft."

Annora took no offense at his slightly suggestive tone but held her ground. "There are plenty of blankets. I'll make a pallet in the girls' room, and—"

A raising of his hand cut her off. "Nice of you to offer, miss, but there's no extra floor space in there."

"Well, perhaps—"

Mr. Brent gave a weary shake of his dark head and grew serious. "Look, the truth is, you should have a place to call your own. Tomorrow I'll see about clearing out the lean-to on the side of the house. It's not big or fancy, but it'll take a narrow bed, and it's private. You can use that as long as you're here."

The last statement sounded a touch unsettling, but Annora didn't want to make any more waves than she had already. She gave a consenting nod. "Whatever you say. I'm only sorry I'm making extra work when I came with the intention of being a help."

When his compelling eyes turned straight on her, she realized how seldom an occurrence that was—how he seemed to put a lot of effort into never quite looking at her. Annora pondered that knowledge in the brief pause before he spoke.

"You know," he admitted, "even though I'd sent all those notices east and was hoping sombody'd show up—I didn't expect anyone actually would, especially without giving me time to prepare. I should have been ready in case." The hint of a smile emerged. "And you are a help, I can't deny that. A man almost forgets what it's like to have a. . .to have—someone—looking after his house."

Taking the comment as a compliment, she warmed under it.

"So, for the rest of the month, the lean-to will have your name on it." With a decided nod, he turned and left.

The warmth she'd felt quickly evaporated, and she stood where she was, staring after him. *You must be extremely sure I'm not going to work out, aren't you? Well, you must never have met a determined woman before.*

Throwing back her shoulders, Annora moved to clear the table.

eleven

"Close your eyes," Melinda said, taking Annora's hand.

"It's a surprise." Amy slipped her tiny fingers into Annora's other hand, and the two girls led her away from the well where she had gone to draw water for cooking.

"How can I see anything with my eyes closed?" Annora teased as she gingerly navigated the unseen, uneven ground under the warm Wyoming sunshine.

"I'll tell you when you can look," Melinda replied.

Annora did her best to retain a puzzled expression but surmised they were taking her to the lean-to, which had been the source of a considerable amount of hammering, sawing, and muffled mutterings throughout the morning. Her suspicions proved correct when the girls stopped a short distance later and a door squeaked open.

"Surprise!" the little ones chorused.

Opening her eyes, Annora saw that the simple structure abutting the house had, indeed, been turned into a room for her. It appeared a mite cramped, and its dirt floor rendered it even less elegant than her attic quarters in Philadelphia, but at least it was private.

She surveyed the plain narrow cot with the washstand next to it, noting a newly cut window in the side wall that would provide her with light. The interior was fragrant with the scent of the new wood Mr. Brent had used to make shutters. Surely her presence here would no longer seem such an imposition on everyone now that she had a place of her own!

"Like it?" towheaded Amy asked.

Annora ruffled the child's golden hair. "It's fine. Just fine. It'll do quite nicely, I'm sure."

"There's extra blankets in the trunk in Pa's room," Melinda announced.

"Good. I'll get my bed made up for later. Want to help bring out my things?"

The better part of the next half-hour saw the three parading back and forth between there and the house, readying the new quarters for occupancy. When the last of her possessions had been transferred, Annora excused the girls to run and play while she made up her bed.

Just as she finished, a shadow fell across the room's interior. She had not heard approaching footsteps but looked up to see Noah leaning against the doorjamb, his expression unreadable.

"Probably not quite what you're used to," he said.

Choosing to ignore the quality of familiarity in the young man's gaze, Annora smiled. "Oh, it's more than adequate. I appreciate all the trouble this caused you and Mr. Brent."

He shrugged offhandedly. "Actually, it—"

"Don't you have some chores to finish up?" his brother's voice interrupted from behind him.

One side of Noah's mouth tightened, and he turned his eyes upward. "Yes, sir," he said, snapping around with overplayed compliance. He wheeled about and strode away in a huff.

Mr. Brent came closer and peered inside. "We'll try to get a proper floor in here in the next couple days," he said, his tone apologetic, "plus make sure it won't be drafty at night."

Annora gave a cursory nod as she watched his glance roam the limited space. He had taken to shaving every morning, and she couldn't help but notice how much younger he appeared, despite a persistent five o'clock shadow that resurfaced by midday. Still, she was far from comfortable in his commanding presence, and she switched her attention to the immediate area around her before her thoughts wandered any further.

"Have to make a trip into town tomorrow," her employer

said after a short lapse of silence, "to take another load of potatoes to the store and pick up a couple of mares due to come in on the train. You're welcome to tag along and pick out some yard goods for a curtain."

"Thank you. I'd like that very much." Her subdued answer belied the sheer delight caused by the opportunity of going to some actual shops.

"We'll make a day of it, then. It'll be a treat for the girls."

"Shall I make a basket lunch?"

Mr. Brent shook his head. "We'll leave after breakfast and pick up something while we're there."

ૐ

After a surprisingly restful night in her new bed, Annora rose early and dressed, then enjoyed some quiet moments in prayer before starting breakfast. She had heard the farmer exit the kitchen door a short time ago and assumed he was seeing to his morning routine, which included taking the stallion for his usual daily workout.

The girls were still in bed when she went inside, but their quiet whispers and darling giggles carried easily to Annora's ears. She knew the little ones had to be excited about the planned outing. Tiptoeing to their open doorway, she peeked in at them, catching their bright smiles. "Good morning, sweethearts."

Melinda sprang to a sitting position. "We're goin' to town today."

"All of us," her sister added. "You, too, Pa says."

"That's right. So how about washing up and putting on your prettiest dresses," Annora suggested. "And don't forget to make your bed."

"Aw. . .are we gonna haveta do that every day?" the older child asked. "Pa never made us."

"Well, that's because you were just little girls up until now. But since you've been helping with chores so nicely, you're starting to become young ladies."

"Ladies?" Amy sputtered into a giggle. "Like Miss Rosemary?"

Melinda poked her in the ribs. "No, silly. She said *young ladies*. That means—" She thought for a second. "—big girls. Right?" The questioning expression she raised to Annora was almost comical.

"Right." Annora was hard pressed to contain a smile. "And even better, it shows you have love in your heart. That's what families do. Each person helps the other, then everybody is happy."

A dubious glance passed between them, then the older sibling nodded. "Happy is nice. We'll make the bed. Come on, Sissy."

As the two settled to their task, Annora returned to the kitchen to strain the pail of fresh milk on the sideboard and prepare breakfast. But reminded again of the elusive Miss Rosemary, her curiosity was piqued.

After the family finished eating and the kitchen had been set to rights, Lucas Brent went to hitch up the wagon. The girls wasted no time in jumping aboard. Annora climbed up with proper decorum, only to discover she would either have to sit between the two Brent brothers or ride in back with the girls. When she chose the latter, her employer clucked the workhorses forward.

The Indian summer day added gentle beauty to the open countryside, and soft breezes stirred the drying grasses and fading vegetation as the wheels crunched along the rutted road.

While Melinda and Amy giggled over the excitement of going to town, Annora watched the play of sunlight against Mr. Brent's muscular shoulders as he and Noah chatted quietly up front. In his form-fitting jeans, work shirt, and Stetson, the farmer fit in naturally with this open, untamed country. She could not even imagine him in a proper dark suit, confined behind a desk in some city office.

Nevertheless, Annora had dismissed immediately upon arriving at the Brent farm the farfetched notion of this position ever leading to marriage. Truth was, she was in no hurry to wed anyone—ever—especially a man much older than she. All she wanted was for this trial period to work out so she could stay until a better opportunity presented itself. She was determined never to return to Philadelphia as long as she lived! Pressing her lips together in confirmation, she diverted her attention to the passing landscape, catching an over-the-shoulder glance from Noah as she did so. It was not the first she'd noticed in the last couple days, but she paid him no mind.

Cheyenne, never peaceful or idyllic even at the best moments, was its normal bustling self, with a liberal assortment of humanity thronging the dusty streets between business establishments. Reading the hand-painted signs identifying those the wagon passed, Annora was mildly surprised when Mr. Brent halted the team before, of all places, a millinery.

He turned to her. "I have to pick up some mending we left here last time. You might as well come in. After that, I'd appreciate it if you'd ride herd on the girls while Noah and I take care of business."

"Of course."

"Think I'll check with the postmaster while the rest of you go in there," Noah announced, helping Melinda down while Annora handed Amy to her father.

Wondering if word would come soon from another applicant for her position, Annora quashed her uneasiness, then allowed Mr. Brent to lower her to her feet. She purposely did not permit herself to reflect upon how strong his touch had felt upon her waist but joined him and his daughters as they clomped over the wooden walkway to the store's entrance.

A small bell above the door tinkled as they went inside, the sound bringing a slim young woman from the back room. Petite in stature, she was scarcely an inch taller than Annora and was impeccably attired in a rich shade of sapphire that accented the flawless, fair complexion beneath her coronet of golden braids. The few wispy hairs that formed curls alongside her face only added to the delicacy of her feminine features.

"Good day, Miss Rosemary," the little ones singsonged.

"Girls." The polite smile curving the lady's lips split into a warm grin as her shrewd hazel eyes settled on Mr. Brent. "Lucas." They narrowed almost imperceptibly when they came to Annora.

"Rosemary," the farmer said, tipping his hat. "Thought I'd stop by for the mending."

"I see. It's in back. I'll just be a moment." Flicking another glance in Annora's direction, she went through the curtain panels separating the main room from the work area and returned seconds later. "You have company?" she asked pointedly, handing him a wrapped parcel.

"Miss Annora's our new housekeeper," Melinda said proudly.

"*Housekeeper*." The bonnetmaker's tone fairly dripped with incredulity.

"She's been sleepin' in Pa's room," Amy elaborated. "But Uncle Noah helped him build a new one for her."

Annora felt her face flush with the implication that could be taken from Amy's innocent comment and thought she detected a noticeable ruddiness about Mr. Brent's neck as he shifted his weight from one foot to the other.

He cleared his throat. "I'd like you to meet Annora Nolan, Rosemary. She's from the East. Came in answer to my notice. Annora, this is Rosemary Evans, a friend of ours."

"I'm pleased to make your acquaintance, ma'am," Annora said, mustering her friendliest smile.

The woman stared in cool appraisal momentarily, then she gave a perfunctory nod. "*Housekeeper*," she repeated in disbelief. "Now I've heard everything."

Trying very hard not to be offended by the less-than-enthusiastic greeting or the insinuation behind it, Annora chewed the inside corner of her lip and averted her attention to some of the fashionable hats on display stands about the room.

Mr. Brent finally responded. "Yes, well," he said with a shrug, "thanks for taking care of these. I'll settle up with you when I get back from the bank."

Mildly annoyed that he hadn't bothered to explain, Annora stole a quick glance through her lashes at the store's owner.

If Rosemary Evans was put off by his obvious omission, she concealed the fact. "No hurry. I trust you, Lucas. You should know that by now."

He nodded, then offered his free hand to his younger daughter. "Come on, pumpkin. We'll let Miss Rosemary get back to work. How about you and Melinda showing Annora around while your uncle and I see to business?"

"Oh, goodie," Amy said, raising her adoring gaze to him.

Claiming Melinda, Annora followed her employer to the door, aware of those icy eyes watching her departure. She was relieved to step back out into the sunshine once more. But the chilly reception she had received from the bonnetmaker stole some of the enjoyment from Annora's day—especially when a passing glance or two at the millinery during the next hour or so revealed the Evans woman staring out at her. Realizing the lady must actually view her as a rival for Mr. Brent's attentions, Annora shook her head, sloughing off the ludicrous possibility.

ح

Later that night, after the weary girls had been tucked into bed, and the men had gone to the barn to look after the new horses, Annora sought the sanctuary of the lean-to.

Neatly folded atop her coverlet lay the yard goods she'd chosen. She picked up the material and shook it out, then held the fabric up to the window. The bright yellow calico would definitely add cheer to the dismal room, she decided with satisfaction. Setting it aside, she gazed at her other purchase, one which a small amount of her remaining traveling funds had provided—a supply of writing paper. She had only begun to realize how much she missed Lesley.

After lighting the bedside lamp, Annora sat cross-legged on her cot and smoothed a sheet of paper over the lap desk she had borrowed from the house. She thought for a moment, then began writing:

Dear Lesley,

It seems ages since I last set eyes upon that smiling face of yours. I missed you from the onset and thought of you throughout my long, exhausting rail journey. The Lord did provide me with a rather nice woman friend on the train, but I will elaborate on her another time. There is far too much other news to tell you just now.

I pray you and Michael did not suffer undue consequences for my fleeing Philadelphia. My conscience still pricks over having deceived my guardians, as I know they truly meant well. Nevertheless, I am convinced I made the right choice in coming to Wyoming.

This farm is several miles outside Cheyenne, so I had to get used to being somewhat apart from even that limited amount of civilization. I do like the open country, especially at sunset, when the whole sky is ablaze with vivid color.

I must admit, my sudden appearance here caught everyone off guard. Somehow my letter had gotten waylaid, so I actually arrived before my missive. It made things a bit awkward at first, but I pleaded for Mr. Brent to give me a month in which to prove myself. If that works out, I shall be satisfied to remain here indefinitely. I am not entertaining the slightest notion of someday marrying the man. He seems a decent sort but is somewhat older. I also believe there is a woman in town who has designs on him.

I do love his little girls, however. Melinda and Amy

are adorable. They seem to enjoy having someone
around to read to them and spend time with them, but at
the same time, they show a natural possessiveness
about their late mother's things. Once their father
assured them I am here only temporarily, they were
more able to accept my presence.

Tapping her pencil against her teeth in thought, Annora debated whether to mention Noah, then continued:

> *Mr. Brent's younger brother, Noah, also lives here on*
> *the farm. He does not impress me as much more than a*
> *shiftless prankster, but he is quite handsome. No doubt*
> *he turns a few heads among the eligible young women*
> *in town, but he has not spoken of any in particular.*
> *We have not as yet attended Sunday services. That*
> *does feel strange, after having almost lived at church*
> *during the past three years. I shall inquire about going*
> *this week's end. Surely my employer is concerned about*
> *the eternal fate of his daughters' souls.*
> *In case you have no time to spend reading overlong*
> *letters, I shall close for now. But please know, dear*
> *Lesley, that I shall perish unless I hear from you soon.*
> *Until then, do take care. Give Michael my warmest*
> *regards, and may the Lord bless you always.*
>

With deepest affection,
I remain your friend,
Annora
>

Scanning the entire letter through, Annora folded it and tucked it into an envelope to be ready for delivery on the next trip to town. But it took awhile for the pang of homesickness for her best friend to subside.

Annora could not help wondering if she would ever feel at home anywhere, ever again.

twelve

Annora's immersion into the backlog of household duties made the next week pass quickly for her. Harvest and its related field work had all but come to an end, along with the long laborious hours of backbreaking toil that normally occupied the men during the warm weather. Mr. Brent was free to turn his attention to other matters—and with the acquisition of the two mares he'd sent for, his high spirits lent a more buoyant air to the atmosphere around the farm.

His optimism spilled over onto his daughters, who now helped willingly with daily household chores in return for horseback rides with their father. Annora decided not to let the girls' cheerfulness go to waste. Concluding that her employer wouldn't deem it a proper use of time to drive to the school in Cheyenne every day until both children were old enough to enroll, she planned to start spending part of their story-reading sessions teaching them the alphabet.

One afternoon, while taking down some wash, Annora caught a glimpse of Mr. Brent putting Chesapeake through his paces. Curious, she went to the corral fence and climbed up on a low rung to watch, fascinated by his skill and his obvious love for the spirited mount. She couldn't help but admire the beautiful reddish-brown horse with its black mane, tail, and points.

"They're something, ain't they?" Noah, just back from town, took the spot next to her, chewing absently on the stem of a long weed he had quirked in one corner of his mouth. His shirt sleeve rested against Annora's bare arm.

Uncomfortable at his nearness, she shifted her weight slightly away from him. "I've never seen prettier horses," she answered casually, her sweeping glance including the mares serenely exploring an adjacent section of the corral. One was a black color with a silky mane and tail, and the other, gray with speckled hindquarters. Even the workhorses were fine-looking creatures and had temperaments almost as pleasant as the milk cow grazing in the pasture.

"Well, if there's one thing that brother of mine is a good judge of, it's horseflesh. This is the beginning of his grand dream, you know."

"Oh?" Annora turned toward the young man.

"Yep. All this farmin', it's just been a means to an end. Sale of the excess crops to the local stores has provided capital he's been needin' to buy stock. With all the big cattle spreads in the territory, he figures there'll be a steady market for good, trained mounts in the future. He wants to raise 'em."

Annora returned her attention to the working pair. "Is that your dream, too?"

Noah gave a derisive snort. "Nah. If I ever get wind of a new gold strike anywhere, I'm off to parts unknown. Don't have the patience Lucas has, to spend years and years developing a herd of prize stock." Removing his wide-brimmed hat, he used it to point with as he blotted his forehead on his other sleeve. "Take old Ches, now. He has enough thoroughbred in him to make him fast. Real fast. Meanwhile, his pacer blood makes him agile. And the mares, they're strong and sturdy. Should make a good combination of qualities for cattle ponies. Course, Lucas'll keep adding to his breeding stock, too, as his finances allow."

Contemplating the information while Noah replaced his hat, Annora admired the sorrel's fluid movements—to say nothing of those of his owner. They moved and worked as one, the beautiful animal responding to the slightest flick of the rein from his master.

"Do you ride?" Noah asked suddenly.

"Me?" she asked with a light laugh. "No. I've never been around horses much."

"I'd be glad to teach you sometime." A provocative smirk tugged at his mouth.

Somehow, surmising he had other things in mind besides mere riding lessons, Annora heard an alarm bell go off in her head. She hopped down from the fence rail. "Thanks." She brushed the fence dust from her hands. "But I doubt there'll be a chance for anything like that in the near future. I don't have much time left, you know, before my trial month is up."

He slanted her a lopsided grin, his blue eyes gleaming. "What makes you think you won't get the job permanent?"

"I haven't heard anything that would make me think so."

"Well, now, you just never know, do you?" He cast a glance in his brother's direction, did a double-take, and sobered.

Annora noticed Mr. Brent eyeing the two of them.

Noah turned and started for the barn, then stopped. "Oh. By the way. Almost forgot. Postmaster gave me this for you." He reached inside his vest pocket and held a letter out to her.

"Truly?" Her heartbeat quickened as she unceremoniously grabbed the envelope. Recognizing Lesley's handwriting, she concluded that her own letter and Lesley's had probably crossed somewhere en route. She dashed to her private quarters and tore open the treasure, scanning its contents.

Dear Annora,

I am sending this in care of Mr. Brent in the hope that it will find you. I knew I would miss you, but I had no idea exactly how empty this great city would seem after you left. I do pray you are faring well out in the wilds, but never forget that you do have a home back here among your friends, should you find yourself in dire straits.

You must be wondering what happened at the church after your hasty departure. From what I heard, the sanctuary was absolutely packed with an expectant audience as the flustered, perspiring groom came to wait for his

*nonexistent bride to walk down the aisle. When you did
not appear, the Baxters were beside themselves. After
dismissing the crowd, they set up an immediate meeting
with Percy's solicitors to see what could be done to fore-
stall having his inheritance tied up in a trust fund for the
next twenty-five years. Finally, in an effort to save face,
it was decided that Mirah would marry Percival when
she turns sixteen. How I would have loved to have seen
the brat's face when the news was presented to her! She's
always had such high and lofty intentions.*

At this unforeseen turn of events, Annora was overcome by
giggles and laughed until she had to hold her sides. So Mirah
Baxter had gotten her *comeuppance* after all, just as Mrs.
Henderson had predicted! When her mirth subsided, she
shook her head and continued reading:

*I do hope things have worked out in your favor regard-
ing your position in Wyoming. The moment you have
time to take pen in hand, I hope you will go into great
detail about your new home, your employer, and his
children. Until then, know that you are constantly
in my prayers. Michael joins me in wishing you every
happiness.*

> *Your friend always,*
> *Lesley*

Blinking unexpected moisture from her eyes, Annora
hugged the missive to her heart, then reread it through from
the beginning. Lesley had given no indication of having been
implicated in Annora's flight to the West. With a great sigh of
relief, she lay back on her bed and smiled.

Her reverie met a swift end with a knock on her door.

"Miss Annora?" Melinda asked. "When's supper?"

"I was just about to start on it, sweetheart." Rising, Annora folded Lesley's letter and tucked it inside the envelope once more, then put it under her pillow for later readings.

☙

Annora ladled portions of rich venison stew into everyone's bowls, then lowered herself to the chair and bowed her head. "We thank You, dear Lord, for Your wondrous provision and bounty. Please bless this meal and use it to our sustenance and us to Your service. Amen."

Gratified that her custom of saying grace at mealtimes had so easily become an accepted practice here, she slathered butter onto a thick slice of bread and bit off a chunk as she worked up courage to broach yet another questionable topic.

Mr. Brent and Noah, apparently more hungry than talkative this evening, made quick work of their first helpings, then refilled their bowls and dug in again.

Annora swallowed. "Tomorrow's Sunday."

The silence bracketing that pronouncement was so profound, her words seemed to ring in the air.

Melinda and Amy looked at her, then at their father, whose face registered nothing whatever.

"And I was wondering," Annora plunged on, "if we could start attending services."

Her employer filled his lungs and slowly exhaled. "Not much point in that," he said flatly with barely a pause in his eating.

Refusing to be cowed by his attitude, she pressed on. "No point in worshipping God?"

Lucas Brent set down his spoon and met her gaze straight on. "Look, miss. We used to put a lot of store in that truck. Now we get along just fine without it. Besides, there's work that needs doing. We can't be traipsing off to town all the time."

"But it would be good for the girls to—"

His demeanor hardened, as did the steel blue of his eyes. He opened his mouth to speak, but his brother beat him to it.

"I could drive 'em in on Sundays," Noah piped up.

"Forget it. If we go someplace like church, it's either all of us or none."

Annora didn't quite know what to make of that statement.

"We used to go to meetin' every Sunday," Amy said in a tiny voice, "when Mama was here. She said it was 'portant."

Some of the resolve tightening Lucas Brent's lips appeared to lessen. "I don't want to talk about this right now." He rose and shoved his chair back with his legs, but before he could take his leave, the child's rounded azure eyes shimmered with tears. "I'll. . .think on it," he muttered. "But don't count on tomorrow." With that, he crossed the room and stomped out.

Annora flinched as the door banged shut behind him.

Noah just grinned. "Well, well. It would appear somebody's startin' to get through to Big Brother."

But it was much too soon to count her employer's weakening stance a victory, Annora knew. As she cleaned up after the meal and readied the girls for their bedtime, she felt far from easy about having confronted the man right under the noses of his children. The least she could do was apologize.

She had been around long enough to perceive that whenever the farmer seemed particularly tense, he spent extra time with his beloved Chesapeake. The bond between the horse and the man was almost tangible, even to a casual observer. So when the opportunity at last presented itself, she made her way to the barn.

"He's very beautiful," she said quietly, approaching the stall. Tentatively, shyly, she reached to touch the velvety face, surprised at how soft and warm it was as the animal nuzzled against her palm.

Her employer's dark head turned, and he looked at her but did not speak.

Lowering her hand, she settled back onto her heels and fidgeted a little, toying nervously with the edge of her apron. "I came to say I'm sorry, Mr. Brent. I didn't mean to cause a scene at the supper table."

He leaned his forearms on the horse's rump and cocked his head, regarding her with those penetrating eyes of his. "Don't you think it's about time you dropped the 'mister' bit?" he asked simply. "Makes me feel like I'm my dad. My friends call me Lucas."

It was the last thing Annora would have expected him to say. Not sure of how to respond, she drew her lips inward and lightly bit down on them.

"After all that grace saying, I should have known it was only a matter of time till you brought up going to church. Must be a woman thing."

Annora tucked her chin. "You don't mean that."

"No. . .I guess I don't," he admitted reluctantly.

Something about the way he'd said it—or was it the honesty behind it?—gave Annora hope, and she felt herself relax a notch as he went back to brushing the reddish-brown hide.

"It was pretty important to my wife," Lucas went on. "To both of us, actually. But when she died, I. . ." Though his words trailed off, the pain they etched into his tanned features quite eloquently finished the thought.

Annora nodded with understanding and silently prayed for wisdom before she replied. "It's. . .hard to part with someone you love. Hard to understand the whys. . .especially when they don't make a lick of sense."

He appeared to consider the comment as he kept working, and a corner of his mouth twitched, but he didn't quite smile. His gaze sought hers again, as if reading her innermost thoughts. "Yeah, I guess if anybody knows what it's like to be left alone, it'd be someone like you."

"You get used to it," she said softly. "Anyway, I have never been completely alone. The Lord has always been there for me."

His movements stopped. "Then, why do you suppose He delights in snatching a mama away from young'uns who need her?"

Annora thought for a minute. "I don't think He *delights* in it. At least, not in the way you mean. The Bible says the death of His saints is a very precious thing to Him. . .a reward, if you will, to His faithful ones. And it says that all our days are numbered before we are even born. We're the ones who think everybody is entitled to that three-score years and ten it talks about."

A wry smile played across Lucas's mouth as he shook his head in contemplation, the lantern's glow making silver highlights against his brown-black hair. "Never thought about it quite that way." Hanging the brush on a hook, he patted Chesapeake's muscular neck and exited the stall, latching it after him. "Don't suppose there's any more of that good coffee we had at supper."

"Sure is. And it goes perfectly with the apple pie."

He grinned unabashedly. "One thing's for sure, Annora. You know your way around a kitchen."

"It's something else I got used to, awhile back."

"Well then, maybe I'll trouble you for some pie and coffee . . .if it won't make us oversleep for church tomorrow."

The surprising words all but sang across Annora's heartstrings. This truly was a victory. . .and a joyous one, at that. A smile broke forth. "Not at all. . .Lucas."

thirteen

Lucas hadn't intended ever to darken church doors again after Francie's funeral. How on earth he had allowed his little red-headed housekeeper to coerce him into coming to service today would forever remain a mystery. But here he was.

He had dawdled about, taking his good-natured time parking the wagon while the rest of the family went inside. Now through the partially open windows the first wheezy notes from the pump organ drifted to his ears.

Might as well get this over with. Filling his lungs, Lucas wiped his sweaty palms on his pant legs, trudged up the familiar steps, then before he changed his mind, strode purposely through the vestibule.

The very second his boot heels echoed on the plank floor, every individual present turned to gawk. Lucas shut out the volley of hushed whispers and the amazed expressions making the rounds. They were the least of his woes. . . . Noah had led the family to the first pew, clear up front! Grinding his teeth in consternation, he made a solemn vow. *That kid brother of mine better be on speaking terms with his Maker. When I get him home, I'm gonna wring his scrawny neck!*

Feigning nonchalance, Lucas marched the length of the center aisle to join his kin. And all the way, he tried to convince himself it was his imagination that the tempo of the prelude matched the rhythm of his steps.

He crossed in front of Noah—who purposely avoided the look intended to sear him to his bones—crossed in front of the girls, then Annora, taking the next spot on the hard bench. He was still seething when Rosemary Evans came from the opposite aisle and plunked herself down beside him, a brilliant smile on her face as she settled her yellow taffeta skirts about her.

The musical piece ended on a sustained final note, and the Reverend Miles Gardner stepped to the pulpit. The gray-haired minister's round face fairly beamed as his gaze finally moved from Lucas to include the other worshipers. "My dear brothers and sisters," he began. "This is a day of great celebration. Let us bow our hearts before our Holy God."

Lucas was so busy plotting his brother's demise, he missed all but the closing "Amen." But since he'd made that drive into town expressly for the worship service, he'd see it through. He crossed his arms and focused his attention on the minister even as Rosemary inched closer.

❧

There weren't many similarities between this small clapboard church and the grand brick one where the Reverend Baxter served, Annora decided. Clear windows rather than stained glass, plain pulpit instead of one ornately carved, and many of the folks who had come this morning were dressed quite simply. A few men even wore what appeared to be work clothes. But everyone's smiles had seemed genuine when she and the girls had traipsed down the aisle behind Noah.

Drawing comfort from the familiar hymns and the friendly atmosphere of the rustic frontier church, Annora purposely avoided returning any of the pointed looks the bonnetmaker occasionally threw her way. It had been weeks since she'd last had the privilege of being in Sunday services, and Annora looked forward to feasting again on the Word of God. When the minister stepped to the pulpit, something about his demeanor assured her that her spirit would not go away unsatisfied.

The pastor's kindly brown eyes surveyed the small congregation, and he smiled. "Brothers and sisters, this will be the third and final message in our series, 'Restoring a Broken Fellowship with God.' "

Beside her, Annora felt Lucas stiffen slightly. She breathed a desperate prayer that he would stay and listen to what the Lord laid upon the minister's heart and that everyone present would benefit from the truths presented.

"You will recall," the pastor went on, "that two weeks ago we learned some of the marks of a backslider—including, among other things, no interest in attending church, no desire for Christian fellowship, and no personal time alone with the Lord."

Referring to his notes again, he continued. "And last week we studied some of the reasons why a Christian falls away from his faith—whether it be because of a particular weakness, the result of deep sorrow, or just a gradual cooling toward spiritual matters. But this morning, dear friends, we have not come to focus on the negatives but rather on the glorious positives. I've entitled this sermon 'Coming Home.' Turn with me, if you will, to our text for today, found in the second chapter of Revelation."

The flutter of pages sounded from the few Bibles among the folk present. Annora opened hers and let it rest on her lap.

"This passage," the Reverend Gardner explained as he scanned the audience, "speaks of the church at Ephesus, reminding them that they had left their first love. For whatever reason, they had forgotten the joy of their former days. They had ceased working for the Lord and their zeal had grown cold. But did the Lord give up on them? Not at all. Just look at what the risen Christ tells them to do in verse five: 'Remember therefore from whence thou art fallen, and repent, and do the first works.' We'll look at what those 'first works' entailed—but before we do, let's consider what had to take place beforehand—repentance. . . ."

Annora lost herself in the stirring message, noting how a few of the pastor's gestures and voice inflections reminded her of the Reverend Baxter's manner of preaching. For a few seconds she mentally transported herself back to Philadelphia, imagining she was sharing a pew with Lesley and her other friends. But that fantasy vanished with the realization that if she'd remained in the East, she'd have been sitting with her husband and mother-in-law. A shudder crept up her spine, bringing her attention back to the sermon, which had wound down to the points of application.

When the singing of "Blest Be the Tie That Binds" and a closing prayer brought the service to an end, Noah beat everyone to the exit in his rush to spend the remainder of the day in town with friends. The rest of the worshipers filed out of the pews toward the open double door, where the Reverend Gardner waited to shake hands with his flock.

As a few of the departing folks stopped to chat with Lucas and the girls, Rosemary sidled up to Annora. "So, how's our little housekeeper today?" she asked with a twinge of scorn. "Keeping up with your duties?"

Annora matched the milliner's cool tone. "Yes, as a matter of fact, and discovering what good helpers little girls can be."

"I would imagine." Rosemary's gaze slid to the children, who were absorbed in the chatter going on around them. "Well, perhaps in another year or so, Lucas will take my advice and send them East to be educated. Frontier schools leave much to be desired."

"Personally," Annora countered, "I feel that children need to be with the people who love them. That's far more beneficial than learning needlepoint and Latin."

Rosemary's eyebrows arched higher, then quickly resumed their normal position when she spied Lucas's daughters coming her way.

"Morning, Miss Rosemary," Amy breathed, an angelic smile lighting her face.

"Hello, precious," the milliner cooed, fawning over the young pair. "I've been working on a surprise for both of you."

"For us?" Melinda asked. "A surprise?"

"Mm-hm. It'll be finished real soon."

"Oh, goodie!" Amy hugged the slender woman's waist.

"What's all this?" Lucas asked, coming to join the group.

"Miss Rosemary's making us a surprise," Melinda told him. "She says it's almost finished."

"Well, that's nice, pumpkin." He tousled his daughter's hair and smiled at Rosemary. "I'm amazed you have time to devote to a special treat for the girls, busy as you are with your shop."

"I always have time for the people who matter to me," she replied with a dazzling smile.

"Excuse me, please," Annora murmured, withdrawing from the nauseating performance. The woman was nowhere near as accomplished as Mirah Baxter at feigning sweetness. Besides, all that claw-sharpening served no purpose. Annora's relationship with the farmer was strictly business.

Stepping up to shake the pastor's hand, Annora fought to forget the scene behind her. . .hoping in her heart that the Lord had someone nicer than Rosemary Evans in store for Lucas and his little darlings.

№

After dining on succulent roast beef and mashed potatoes at the Brass Kettle Restaurant, Lucas steered the girls to the waiting rig. Noah had dined with friends of his and would hitch a ride home with them later.

"You might as well ride in comfort," Lucas quipped, assisting Annora up to the seat while his daughters climbed into the wagon bed. Then he loosened the reins from the hitching post and hopped aboard.

Melinda and Amy, who had dominated the conversation in the restaurant by keeping up a lively string of talk during the meal, resumed their girlish chatter and giggling in back. But before the team had covered half the homeward miles, Annora noticed that the pair had grown unaccountably quiet. She peered over her shoulder and discovered they had fallen asleep.

Lucas followed her gaze, then turned his head forward.

Annora studied her nails momentarily, then let out a breath of resignation as the countryside rolled by.

Finally he looked at her, his eyes shadowed by the brim of his Stetson. "Would you call me a backslider?"

"I beg your pardon?"

"You heard me. That was some sermon the reverend lambasted me with."

Annora wanted to smile but knew better. She assumed what she hoped was a pleasant look as she silently sought wisdom from the Lord. "He wasn't lambasting you, Lucas. He didn't even know you'd be there. His message was part of a series he started weeks ago."

"Sure sounded like he aimed it right at me."

"Well, perhaps it wasn't the—" Flushing over almost speaking her mind, Annora tried again. "I mean. . ." In despair, she closed her mouth and averted her gaze.

"Go on and finish what you were saying," he grated. "Couldn't be any worse than what was hurled at me from the pulpit."

After a slight hesitation, Annora moistened her lips and began over. "I was going to say, if it seemed all that personal, perhaps it was the Lord, not the pastor, trying to get your attention."

He stared straight ahead and didn't respond right away. A muscle worked in his jaw. "The Lord got my attention real good not too long ago when he took my wife away from me."

"Had she. . .been sick?" Having actually voiced the question, Annora caught her lip between her teeth. Had she pried into something too deeply personal?

Lucas shook his head. "Francie was. . .in the family way. She was so happy, thinking maybe the Lord was going to give us a son this time. The girls didn't even know about it yet, but we were on the verge of telling them." The beginnings of a bittersweet smile appeared, only to disappear on a ragged breath.

Knowing it must be intensely painful to talk about it, Annora wanted to say she was sorry for asking and that he didn't have to tell her more. But he didn't give her the chance.

"One hot afternoon when I was working out in the field, she took it upon herself to bring me some lemonade. To this day, I don't really know what happened—whether she caught her heel somehow, or stepped in a hole, or just plain tripped. But she fell. Hard. And then the bleeding started. When I heard her cry out, I carried her to the bed and rode for the doc. But by the time we got back, she was—" His voice broke. "She. . ."

It was more than Annora could bear. Without thinking, she took his big, callused hand in her much smaller one and squeezed it in wordless comfort. There was nothing she could say anyway.

A moment or two passed before Lucas withdrew his hand from her grasp. Then before she knew what was happening, his fingers brushed across her cheek, wiping away a tear.

Annora had no idea it had been there until the breeze whispered over the damp streak left behind. That he would be concerned for her despite his own pain provided a small glimpse into the depth of the man's compassion. And the fact that her face still tingled where his fingers had brushed against it sent a surge of indescribable flutterings through her being. Confused over the tangle of emotions within her, she fought the maddening tendency to blush as she looked away.

They rode onward in silence, the jangle of the harness, the clomping of the horses' hooves, and the rattle of the wagon the only sounds.

Lucas was first to speak. "You never answered my question, you know." The lopsided grin he flashed appeared a touch forced, but it helped lighten the moment. "Do you think I'm a backslider?"

Annora, exceedingly grateful for the change of mood, dared to jump in. "Did the shoe fit?"

"Like it was made to order."

She smiled back. "Well, if it's any comfort, there was something in that sermon for all of us, Lucas. Me included."

"Is that so?"

"Mm-hm. For example, that God is sovereign. That the things that happen in our lives don't have to make sense to us, only to Him. And that what matters is how we respond to those circumstances. After all, He has promised to work all things out for our good."

Lucas thought for a few seconds. "For such a young person, you sure sound like a preacher sometimes."

"Maybe because I lived with one after my parents died."

"They die sudden?"

"Barely two weeks apart. Typhoid." Surprisingly, the memory had lost some of its old sting.

He shook his head. "I guess you know about death's cruel blows yourself." And with a smile, he reached for Annora's hand and enveloped it tightly in empathy, holding it for a second timeless moment as they rode along.

Annora derived immense comfort from that tender gesture. But in spite of the way his touch seemed to do strange things to her insides, she reminded herself that nothing was different. Lucas was still her employer and she merely his hired help. But as they came within sight of the farm, she felt that some inner healing had taken place this day. . .in both their hearts.

fourteen

Pastor Gardner's sermon nagged at Lucas for days. He tried to keep busy, but no amount of work could completely erase the things that had been said during—or after—the Sunday service.

A few nights later, after everyone else had gone to bed, he lay in the stillness with his fingers laced together behind his head, staring at the ceiling. Echoes of the minister's words buzzed around in his mind like a persistent insect.

Backslider. What a disagreeable word that was! Rude, even insulting. . .yet excruciatingly true. The term aptly fit a believer who had strayed from the Lord. Whether or not his reasons for turning his back on God had appeared justifiable at the time, Lucas knew there was no excuse for willfully slamming shut the door of his life in the very face of God.

God is sovereign.

The things that happen in our lives don't have to make sense to us, only to Him.

What matters is how we respond to those circumstances.

Annora's quiet melodious voice had given those concepts a gentle logic Lucas could not fault. Odd, the depth of spiritual wisdom that came "out of the mouths of babes," as the Bible said. First, that tiny reminder from Amy about the importance of worshipping the Lord, then the guileless remarks that fell so incredibly easily from Annora's tongue at just the right moment. Reflecting upon the inherent sincerity that seemed so much a part of her, he mulled her comments over in his unrest, examining them from every possible angle.

He contemplated the selfless, giving personality his house-keeper had displayed since arriving on the farm. For someone of her tender age, she had reached a level of maturity far beyond her years. She'd been through a great deal—enough to make a lot of folks bitter. Yet any trace of sadness in those emerald eyes paled behind the glow of her inner peace. . .the same peace that had once been a precious part of his own life.

Lucas rolled onto his side and punched his pillow, trying to find comfort as his conscience and his reason struggled against each other.

Maybe it's too late for me, he mused. *Maybe I've gone too far and could never find my way back. . .even if I wanted to.*

The instant those bleak theories reared their heads, Lucas flatly rejected them. What was that saying his godly parents had tried to instill in his and Noah's hearts all those years? Oh, yes. *God does not forsake His own.* It might even be possible that although he'd tried to run from the Lord, God had kept him in sight the whole time. The possibility was strangely comforting.

Having had a taste of life without God, Lucas was ready to admit it offered nothing but empty hopelessness. Perhaps the Almighty had brought Annora all the way out here just to remind him that God's faithfulness would forever remain constant. Since she had arrived, Lucas's insides felt like a glacier under the summer sun, beginning to warm, slowly melting around the perimeter. Lately he'd even found himself longing for what he'd once taken for granted, to yearn for the "former things" the pastor had mentioned.

A lot of that was because of her.

Too bad her trial month was almost over.

Too bad she had to be so. . .captivating.

What are you thinking, you addlebrain? He railed inwardly. *You're starting to sound like Noah. She's scarcely more than a child. Best to let her go back where she came from before one of us makes a fool of himself.* Lucas was surer now than ever that he shouldn't extend her stay. That would be the wisest course for all concerned.

Grimly he rolled onto his back again and shut his eyes. He dared not think about how he looked forward to every new day again. Or that it was getting hard to focus on something other than that coppery hair, those soft jade eyes. Or about how empty the place would seem if she went away. He only knew he was getting a little too used to having her around, and that was not good. Not good at all.

⁂

The dried apple scones smelled luscious as Annora slid the hot, golden-brown mounds onto a cooling rack. They were sure to complement the cinnamon applesauce at the end of supper. As she placed the hot baking tray into the sudsy water, she heard the girls clatter down the porch steps.

"Somebody's comin', Miss Annora," Melinda called out. "Looks like company!"

Annora moved to the open door.

A visitor was indeed approaching. The classy red wheels of a canopied buggy rolled smoothly down the lane—and driving a splendid chestnut horse was none other than Rosemary Evans.

Annora tightened her lips. "Go get your pa, girls," she told them, retreating back into the kitchen.

A cheery hubbub soon carried to her ears. Determined not to give in to her curiosity, Annora kept at her chores. But before long Amy burst into the house, her childish face alight.

"Look, Miss Annora. Isn't it pretty?" She held out a lovely frock of sky blue organdy. "Miss Rosemary made new dresses for Sissy and me. For church. Sissy's is pink."

Annora stooped down and drew the child close, admiring the flounced hem and ruffled sleeves, the abundance of lace trim. A dress elegant enough to grace even a big city church back East. "Why, it's just beautiful, sweetheart. You're sure to look real pretty next Sunday."

"Pa said Miss Rosemary could stay for supper, too. He said to tell you to set an extra place. He's takin' her to see the new horses." Without waiting for a response, she tugged free and darted outside again, the new frock left behind on a kitchen chair.

Annora's spirit sank. For a full minute she remained where she was. Then slowly she rose and surveyed the tidy house. She had mopped and dusted earlier, so everything looked about as good as it could. It was her own appearance that left much to be desired. Why had she chosen this day to beat the big rug out on the clothesline and polish that big black stove? Those chores had left her feeling grubby to the bone, and she longed for nothing more than to soak in a big luxurious tub like the one the Baxters had—which, of course, did not exist here on the Brent farm.

With a resigned sigh, she untied her soiled work apron and took a basin of warm water out to her room to make what repairs she could in the few private moments before Lucas and his guest would descend upon her for supper.

Within the hour, everyone gathered around the table. Lucas, as always, occupied the head and Noah the foot, leaving one side for the girls, and the other for Annora and Rosemary. As discomfiting as it was for Annora to sit beside the bonnetmaker after bringing the fried chicken and roasted potatoes to the table, the reprieve serving the food provided was a consolation. At least Rosemary wouldn't be eyeing her throughout the meal.

Absorbed in her thoughts, Annora finally realized that everyone was waiting for her to ask the blessing. She moistened her lips and bowed her head. "Thank You, most gracious Heavenly Father, for giving us these rich stores from Your bounty. Please bless this food and allow us another day to serve You. Amen."

"My," Rosemary gushed as she looked up, "you must have been in the kitchen all day, Amanda."

"Annora," she corrected.

"Oh. Of course. My mistake."

"Actually, we've been eatin' real good since Annora got here," Noah piped up.

"She even makes cookies and pies," Melinda added.

"You don't say." The milliner helped herself to a steaming potato from the bowl Lucas passed to her.

"And," Lucas said, "she keeps a neat house. Our little Annora has been a real asset around the place."

Hearing herself all but lumped in the children's category, Annora swallowed her bite of chicken without chewing it. She toyed with the remainder of her food, pushing buttered string beans around her plate while the family chatted with their guest. Thankfully, she reminded herself, she had Lesley to pour her heart out to whenever she felt particularly depressed about anything. It took awhile for letters to go back and forth, but somehow just the writing out of her innermost feelings made dealing with things easier.

". . .and Sissy and me can wear our new dresses."

Amy's voice drew Annora back to reality.

"They're so pretty," the little one went on as she reached for her glass of milk. Halfway to her mouth it slipped from her greasy fingers and tumbled onto the table, flooding the tablecloth and spilling over onto Rosemary's lavender skirts.

"Oh!" the milliner gasped. "My dress!" She sprang to her feet, using her napkin to mop uselessly at the creamy blotches as the girls' mouths gaped in horror.

Lucas rose also but stood helplessly looking on.

"I'll get you a damp cloth," Annora offered. In seconds she returned and handed the clean rag to the disgruntled guest, who was almost in tears over the ruination of her lovely ensemble.

"Sorry, Miss Rosemary," Amy said weakly.

With scarcely more than a pointed glare at the child, the woman continued sponging her skirt.

"Accidents happen," Lucas told his daughter in a consoling tone. He touched Rosemary's shoulder. "Come on, I'll drive you back to town before the stain sets."

"I–I wouldn't want to put you out," she hedged.

"No problem. I'd feel better about it if I at least knew you got home safe. I'll go saddle Chesapeake and tie him behind your buggy."

"Well, I really would appreciate that," she said, warming immediately to the suggestion. "We could continue the conversation we started a little while ago."

He nodded and took her elbow to assist her outside but glanced over his shoulder at his brother. "Make sure the stock is looked after before I get back, will you? I shouldn't be too long."

"Right." Claiming another drumstick from the platter, Noah continued eating as though nothing untoward had happened.

Thoughts of Lucas sharing seven cozy miles with Rosemary Evans was not exactly comforting to Annora, but she knew she had no claims on the farmer herself. He was a grown man and more than able to make his own choices—no matter how unsuitable she might deem them personally. Returning her attention to Melinda and Amy, she noticed they appeared a bit subdued. Annora smiled at them. "Here, let me take your plates, girls. Ready for some applesauce and warm scones?"

They dragged their worried gazes from the doorway their father and his guest had so recently exited.

"Everything will be fine," she said gently. "Miss Evans will wash and iron her dress and it will be good as new. I promise."

Their troubled frowns disappeared, and Amy gave a huge sigh. "I really didn't mean to spill my milk."

"I know, sweetheart. Now, stop fretting. I'll get some dessert, and we'll finish our meal."

Noah chuckled. "Sure can get mad, that one," he said with a tip of his dark head in the direction of the door. "Least little thing, and she's like a chicken that got dunked in the crick."

Melinda sputtered into a giggle, but Annora shot the young man a scathing glower. "Now, now."

"Yes, ma'am," he said in acquiescence. "Must remember not to gloat over somebody else's misfortune, and all that rot." But his mischievous gaze held hers and wouldn't release.

Annora finally looked away. "I'd better clear the table." Telling herself he was naturally forward and didn't mean anything by his ungentlemanly ogling, she hastened to make room for the end-of-meal sweets.

But as the sound of the departing buggy drifted in from the lane, she realized the scones and applesauce no longer held any appeal for her.

※

The sun sank below the horizon, spilling the sky's pastel hues in a muted glow over rocks and bushes in the gathering dusk. Lucas drove the rented buggy toward Cheyenne at an unhurried pace, his spirited sorrel plodding patiently behind.

Rosemary turned toward him. "It was very sweet of you to insist upon seeing me back to town, Lucas."

He shrugged one shoulder but felt no need to comment.

"And I appreciated the supper invitation," she continued. "A pity the evening came to such an abrupt end." Her wistful expression brightened with a glorious smile. "Or perhaps one might term it a blessing, since it provided a chance to spend some extra time alone." She shifted her position slightly, bringing herself a little closer to him.

"You've always been good company," Lucas admitted. "And the girls think the world of you."

"Yes, well, the little darlings are at such an adorable age," she gushed a little too brightly. "Who can resist those girlish . . .charms?"

He grinned appreciatively. "Thanks for the dresses you made them, by the way. They'll count the hours till Sunday."

"Young ladies need to have new pretty things from time to time—especially when they're growing so quickly." She

11ses121

paused, toying with one of the fine curls framing her face. "I must say, I was pleasantly surprised to see you at church last week."

"It was. . .time." But even as he admitted that truth, Lucas had to wonder if he'd ever have gotten around to attending services if it hadn't been for Annora's gentle prodding. The housekeeper had a way about her that made it hard for a man to refuse whatever she asked. . .considering how little she actually did ask.

"You've done an amazing amount of work on your place since my last visit," Rosemary said, cutting into his reverie. "It really looks nice."

"Thanks." Lucas knew that most of his accomplishments were a direct result of having Annora there to look after the domestic end of things. He hadn't known that kind of freedom since Francie's death. Amazingly, rather than the customary tumult caused by thoughts of his loss, an unusual peace settled over him instead.

A sudden breeze rifled the buggy's framework, and Rosemary snuggled nearer. She laid a hand on his sleeve. "Since you've decided to fit church services into your busy life again, why don't we plan a picnic afterward this Sunday, before all the pleasant weather has passed?"

Lucas feasted his eyes on her delicate beauty. The notion did have some merits.

Then she added specifics.

"The four of us, I mean. You, the girls, and me. After all, it's obvious that Noah is completely enamored by your little housekeeper. I'm sure the two of them would appreciate an opportunity for some time together without so many chaperons around."

Lucas turned his attention forward again. A month ago a picnic with Rosemary might have been a trifle more tempting. But at the moment, he wasn't all that sure he was ready to encourage the bonnetmaker's attentions. . .to say nothing of the hazards of giving his younger brother liberties with Annora that had purposely been withheld until now. "Oh, I don't know, Rosemary," he hedged. "A lot depends on the weather and other things."

"But will you at least think about it?" She swept a yearning look at him through her lashes. "For the sake of the girls? They're getting a little too attached to your maid—whose time there, as I understand it, is almost over."

Rosemary was trying to shove him into a corner, he realized as he made an effort to retain his casual demeanor. "I'll think about it," he mumbled, then clammed up so she'd quit talking.

Lucas needed no reminder of the passage of Annora's trial period. But somehow, hearing those words from someone else sent a cold jolt of reality through him. How could a month have flown by so fast?

fifteen

After Annora read the girls a story and tucked them in bed, she finished straightening the kitchen and went out to her quarters. Lucas had not returned from town as yet, which disturbed her more than she cared to admit. But keeping in mind that her employer was old enough to choose his own special friends, she lectured herself on the hazards of becoming overly concerned with the man's personal affairs.

But does it have to be Rosemary? Recalling the vexatious glare the bonnetmaker had leveled on poor Amy after the unfortunate accident with the milk, Annora had to wonder what sort of a stepmother the woman would make—assuming Lucas was considering establishing a permanent relationship with her. Surely other far more suitably eligible females were in town. Perhaps now that he had taken the first step in attending church again, someone more pleasant might catch his eye.

You have no right to be jealous of her, an inner voice pointed out.

Jealous! Annora gave a disdainful huff. *Why, I have never been jealous of anyone in my entire life.*

Not even Mirah? On the day of the picnic? her conscience persisted.

"Well, that was different," she muttered under her breath. "Mirah was after Jason." The remembrance of that past disappointment appeared trivial in the light of her current circumstances. Annora shook her head in astonishment; she had severed so many emotional ties upon leaving Philadelphia, the doctor's son had scarcely entered her mind since the day of her departure. After all, she assured herself, Jason was nowhere near as mature or compelling as. . .Lucas Brent.

What are you thinking? Annora felt her cheeks flame with guilt. All those fluttery sensations that teased her insides in his presence, the peculiar need she felt to restore what he'd lost, the simple joy she found in watching the care lines softening around his eyes whenever he spent time with Melinda and Amy. . .were those proper feelings for a mere housekeeper?

Taking a closer look at them in the quiet solitude of her room, Annora had to admit that no, they were not. In fact, if anything, they were quite the opposite.

She could no longer avoid the truth. The impossible had happened. Somewhere along the way, she had grown to love Lucas Brent. With the inward admission of that surprising truth, Annora's heart soared into the darkening sky. . .only to plunge immediately back to earth like a falling star. It was all for naught. Lucas thought of her as one more little girl.

Well, there was nothing she could do to alter her age. Or his. But one thing she could do was keep these newfound feelings to herself for the remainder of her time here—which she now realized she must terminate on her own when the final day arrived. No use in setting herself up for real heartache.

As always, when beset by things beyond her control, Annora reached for her Bible and opened it to the Psalms. A sound interrupted her, and she glanced up at her door just as someone rapped.

"Annora?" Noah asked.

Wondering what might have brought the young man to her lean-to, she lay the Scriptures aside and got up to open the latch. "What is it?"

The expression he wore seemed a curious blend of mystery and mischief as his lips slid into a lazy smile. "I, er, need you to sew a button on this for Sunday. That is, if you would be so kind." He held out a striped shirt.

"Oh. Of course. I'd be happy to take care of it, Noah. I don't suppose you saved the button, by any chance?"

He shook his head, his eyes imprisoning hers.

"Oh, well, I'm sure Mrs. Brent must have had a button tin. I'll check with the girls tomorrow." Smiling, she turned to set the garment down while Noah took his leave.

He didn't leave.

He followed her inside, giving the door a slight kick with his boot. It clicked shut.

Slanting him a glance, Annora felt little prickles of alarm skitter up her arms. "Is there something else?"

"You might say that."

She gave a perfunctory nod. "Well, tell me what it is. I'm rather busy just now."

"Are you?"

Annora leveled a stare on him, hoping she appeared more confident than she actually was. She opened her mouth to rattle off a list of duties needing her attention, then thought better of it. She didn't have to answer to her employer's younger brother. When he took a bold step closer, she inched backward, knowing she was quickly running out of room in the tiny lean-to.

Still regarding her with that too-penetrating gaze of his, Noah reached out and took a tendril of Annora's long hair, toying with it in his fingers, feathering it past his nostrils. "Nice," he murmured. "Soft, like you. Smells real pretty."

Annora pulled free and set her shoulders. "Stop it, Noah. You've brought me the shirt. Fine. I'll fix it for you. Now, please go."

"Why?" he crooned suggestively, cocking his head to one side. "For once in our lives, nobody is around to order us to go here, do this, do that. Why don't you and me get to know each other a bit?"

"No. It's not proper," Annora retorted.

"But I'm sure a city gal like you must know your way around." He leaned so close his warm breath feathered her neck.

Startled, shocked at his brazen attitude, she placed her hands on his chest and shoved with all her might.

Noah yelped in reflex as he toppled over the corner of her cot. He scrambled to his feet again, rubbing his backside. A lopsided grin added a dangerous gleam to his eyes. "So, that's how you wanna play it. . ."

"Noah!" she scolded forcefully, her arms out in front of her like a shield. "Stop this. You're scaring me. Think about what you're doing."

"What I'm doing," he drawled, "is just—"

The door burst open. Lucas towered in the portal's space.

Annora had not heard her employer return, but she was never so relieved to see anyone in her entire life. Completely unaware of how frightened she had actually been, she felt her knees give way, and she sank onto her bed.

"I told you to keep your hands off her!" she heard Lucas bellow as he yanked his brother bodily outside. "But no, the minute I turn my back, you're all over her like fleas on a dog."

"So what?" Noah returned defensively. "You expect us to believe you didn't just get done smoochin' with Rosie? I figure I'm entitled to—"

One well-directed blow sent the younger man sprawling.

Annora, utterly stunned by the unexpected altercation, could only gawk in horror as Noah crawled to his unsteady feet, rubbing his jaw. He shot a sizzling glower at Lucas, then without further word, he spun on his heel and stalked away in the direction of the barn.

Lucas watched him for a few seconds, then turned and entered the lean-to.

Still shaken, Annora didn't quite know how to react. "I–I'm. . .sorry," she stammered.

"There's nothing you need to be sorry about," he said gently, concern making his straight brows all but meet. "If anybody should apologize, it's me—for that dunderhead brother of mine. I can't let him out of my sight for two minutes." He grimaced. "You all right? Did he hurt you?"

Annora shook her head and smiled thinly as she rose. "I'm fine." But her wobbly knees belied her words.

Lucas reached out and clamped his strong fingers around her upper arms, steadying her. "You're fine. Right. Look at you—you're shaking like a leaf." Without further word, he swept her up into his arms and turned for the door.

The fluid motion rendered Annora speechless as a fragment of memory brought another similar moment to her mind. . . one so faint that she wondered if she had only dreamed it on her first night in Lucas's house.

"Come on," he was saying as his long strides carried them to the house, "I'll fix you a cup of tea. It's gonna be all right, Annora. I'll never let him—"

Before he finished the statement—before the fact registered that his heart was hammering every bit as erratically as hers—the clatter of horse hooves broke in on them.

Lucas relaxed his hold a measure and whirled around. "Chesapeake!" he gasped, going rigid with fury. "Noah! You! Noah!" he hollered. "Get back here! Now!"

But the younger man did not so much as slow down as he galloped away.

Annora felt Lucas's shoulders sag, and he mumbled something under his breath as he set her on her feet. She didn't know whether or not to say anything. Besides, even if she could come up with some profound reply, her emotions were so jumbled she couldn't trust her voice. The events of the last several minutes were beyond anything she would ever have dreamed.

"If he harms Ches, I'll tear him limb from limb," Lucas muttered. Staring uselessly up the now-empty lane for a few seconds, he exhaled a whoosh of defeat. Then, as if coming back to his senses, he took Annora's hand and led her through the door and to the table, where he drew out a chair for her.

"Thank you," she breathed.

Neither spoke as Lucas dumped some tea leaves into the pot and added hot water from the kettle atop the stove. His posture and impatient motions more than revealed his controlled agitation—as did the set of his jaw.

A short time later when he crossed the room with two cups of the rich brew, Annora smiled tentatively as she accepted one and watched him sink heavily onto the seat opposite her.

"I. . .I didn't mean to cause trouble for you," she finally managed in the uncomfortable silence.

"You're not the cause of the trouble," he grated. He took a gulp of tea, then set down his mug with a clunk and got up to pace to the door.

Annora felt his worry as she watched him standing there with his fingers in the back pockets of his jeans, gazing helplessly at the darkened lane. "Can't you go after him on one of the mares?"

He shook his head. "They're not saddle-broke. The hothead will mosey home eventually. . .and when he does, I'll be waiting for him."

Not even daring to imagine yet another confrontation between the two men, Annora nibbled her bottom lip. She could only pray that the Lord would take control of the whole mixed-up situation and keep everyone from getting hurt.

Lucas, a decided droop to his bearing, finally went outside, his steps fading as he trudged away.

Annora stood and took the cups to the sideboard before returning to her haven. Aware of her employer's misery and concern for his fine mount, she was too agitated to sleep, but she changed into her night shift and got out the lap desk. Perhaps a visit with Lesley would calm her spirit.

How long she sat cross-legged on her bed, tapping her pencil on that blank sheet of writing paper, Annora couldn't estimate. But after a time, she put away the writing equipment and blew out the lamp, then crawled between the sheet and light blanket on her bed. There she lay with nothing to do but pray.

Another hour or more dragged by. And one more after that one. Finally, the faint sound of horse hooves drifted from far away. Annora thought at first the noise was her imagination, until the hoof falls grew louder. Something about the pattern did not quite seem right, she realized, and she strained to listen more closely.

There it was again. . .that uneven, halting sound. Her heart thudded to a stop.

Apparently Lucas, too, had detected Chesapeake's return. She heard him come running from the barn.

Hoping against hope that nothing was amiss, Annora swung her legs over the side of her cot and slipped into her silk wrapper, tying it hastily about her waist. Then she padded outside barefooted, anxious to put her mind at ease.

But coming within sight of the lane, she saw Lucas was already kneeling at one of Chesapeake's forelegs, and a jolt of alarm shot up her spine. She picked up her pace, realizing that the horse had no rider. Noah was not to be seen.

"What is it, Lucas?" she whispered when she reached his side.

"If I ever set eyes on that no-account brother of mine again, I'll—"

At the flatness of his tone, Annora laid a comforting hand on his shoulder and sank down next to him. *Please, don't let it be bad*, her heart pleaded. *Not that.*

All the breath seemed to leave the farmer's lungs as he stood to his feet and brushed off his pant legs. "He's hurt. It's his front leg."

Deep despair settled over Annora as she rose and moved to one side so that Lucas could accompany his beautiful bay the rest of the remaining distance to the stall. The sight of the horse's ungainly limp brought tears to her eyes, and she swallowed back a sob. "What can I do to help?" she asked around the tightness in her throat.

"An old blanket. Some cold water," Lucas replied over his

shoulder. "I doubt there's any ice left in the root cellar."

"W–will he. . .be all right?"

Lucas did not answer.

sixteen

As lantern light revealed Chesapeake's condition, Lucas groaned internally. Along with the swollen and bruised foreleg, numerous scrapes and scratches marred the horse's right side. The sorrel must have taken a spill. *Well*, he thought with a rueful grimace, *it's probably too much to hope that Ches rolled over my stupid brother when he fell.* Decidedly lacking in charity at the moment, Lucas could not overlook Noah's irresponsibility—which to him seemed the mark of the kid's whole worthless existence. "Galloping out of here in the dark on a horse that's already tired," he grated under his breath, then expelled a lungful of air in disgust.

At the approach of Annora's soft footsteps, he glanced up.

"How's he look?" she asked shyly, holding out a basin of water to him, along with the pathetic remnant of ice she'd uncovered in the root cellar.

Accepting them gratefully, Lucas gave her a thankful nod and set the containers on the ground. "Bad enough to make me want to spit nails. . .but at least he won't need to be put down. No way I could stomach that." He wet a rag and wrung it out, then began gently dabbing at the misshapen injury.

With a small relieved sigh, Annora slid the worn blanket from her shoulders. "Shall I tear some strips?"

He nodded. "Thanks. No reason for you to lose sleep over this, though. You might as well go get some shut-eye."

Annora regarded him with a steady gaze. "I'd just as soon stay, if you don't mind. I was worried about Ches, too."

The comment came as no surprise. Annora's actions since she'd come west more than demonstrated her sincere care for the people she knew. . .and the knowledge made Lucas feel

131

privileged. And very aware of her presence. He swallowed.

"What will you do for his leg?" she asked.

"Rub liniment on it, apply cold compresses, keep it wrapped, keep him quiet till the swelling goes down. I just hope and pray he didn't pull a ligament." The mention of prayer had come of its own accord, and as Lucas flicked a glance at Annora, he caught her smile.

"I'll pray, too. Would you like some coffee?"

"Sounds great. It's likely I'll be at this for some time." *And I'd just as soon not be alone*, he nearly added as she went back to the house. But with all the conflicting feelings assaulting his insides right now, he was real glad he'd been smart enough to keep his mouth shut.

Chesapeake was safe at home now, where Lucas could look after him. And Annora, too, was safe. Noah had not done her any serious harm. *This time*. Reminding himself to relax his jaw, Lucas went back to his task. *There would be no next time*.

ta

Once the coffee was ready, Annora set the pot on a tray, added two mugs and a pitcher of cream, and returned to the barn. She wondered where Noah was, but she knew better than to bring up that sore subject. For now it was enough that the horse had come back. She'd noticed an easing of Lucas's agitation right away. True, he had a long night ahead, but his steely determination and love for the spirited animal would get him through.

Reaching the stall, she set down the tray, filled the mugs, and added cream. She handed one to her employer before sitting down on the straw nearby to sip her own while she tore up the old blanket.

He nodded gratefully, drained the rich coffee in a few successive gulps, then took up swabbing the horse's numerous scratches with clean water and antiseptic.

Watching him work, Annora was fascinated by his hands.

Strong, square, callused, they nevertheless possessed a softness, a gentleness Lucas brought forth whenever needed. She had experienced some of that herself, when he had carried her inside. He'd been every bit as considerate of her as he'd have been of his own daughters. Of course, realizing that another father was about the last thing she wanted right now, she quickly steered her wayward thoughts to another subject. The horse.

Annora saw that the sorrel's huge velvet eyes had lost the confused, frightened glaze she had glimpsed awhile ago. Now in the presence of his master, submitting to those kind ministrations, a quiet acceptance—an infinite trust—seemed to shine in its place. Lucas Brent, Annora conceded, was a man worthy of that depth of trust.

Of their own volition, her eyes sought the farmer again, and she noted that the care lines that earlier had creased his forehead had vanished. His mouth had lost its rigidity, too, giving a softer quality to his lips. She wondered how they would feel if—*You goose!* she railed inwardly. *You've no call to be entertaining such wanton thoughts about Lucas Brent!* In an effort to gather her emotions, she quickly rolled the remaining strips and stacked them in a neat bundle.

She could not help but think back on the events of the evening—the absolute hopelessness and fear that had torn at her when Noah had made his unwelcome advances. If Lucas had not come back when he had, heaven only knows what might have happened. The mere memory made her insides quake.

And yet, she felt nothing but safe around Lucas. He displayed only the utmost courtesy and respect toward her, and despite the difference in their ages, he spoke to her as an equal. Quite a contrast, those two men.

Even as she measured the one against the other, though, she could not escape the knowledge that they were, in fact, brothers. And she had come between them. Painfully so. With her trial period winding down to its final days, she resolved not to do anything to prolong her stay. Sad as she would be to part with Melinda and Amy, who had become incredibly dear to her from the first. . .it would be sadder still never to see Lucas again. But family relationships were important, and she needed to give this one room and time to mend.

With that conviction taking firm root in her heart, she let out a shallow breath and leaned to refill both their cups.

Time went by quietly. No words passed between them, yet she didn't sense he wished her to go, so she stayed. After about an hour, she watched Lucas unroll the bandage wrapping Chesapeake's foreleg and assess it critically. "How's it doing?"

He cocked his head back and forth in thought. "About as well as could be expected, considering." Then he reapplied liniment and a fresh strip of chilled blanket. "Think that's about all we can do tonight," he finally admitted as he finished up. "We'll have a hard enough time functioning tomorrow if we don't catch a few winks." Exiting the stall with the lantern in one hand, he secured the door, then offered his free hand to Annora.

"Thank the Lord he's going to be all right," she breathed, placing her fingers in Lucas's strong grasp and allowing him to assist her up. She was sure it was her imagination that he held on slightly longer than necessary. And she ignored a flurry of heartbeats as they left the barn side by side in that same pleasant, companionable silence.

"Thanks for keeping me company," Lucas said when they reached the door of the lean-to. "Don't mind admitting that would have been a lonely job, if. . ." His words trailed off, and he brushed the backs of his fingertips over her cheek, a weary smile curving his lips.

"I'm. . .just glad Ches will soon be his old self," she managed. She wanted to say more, wanted to respond to that tender gesture. . .but she knew that if she did, it would only make her last days here harder than ever. "Good night, Lucas."

" 'Night, yourself. You're safe now, you know."

"Yes. I know." With a small smile, she took the lantern he held out to her and went inside, her pulse pounding so hard she wondered if he could hear it, too. Without courage enough to meet his gaze, she softly closed the door, then sagged against it as she listened to him striding away.

She was going to need a lot of prayer to bolster her decision to leave this place willingly. . .especially without even a hint of an alternate plan. Where could she go? What would she do? The first thing she would do, she decided as she undid the buttons on her shirtwaist, was pour her heart out to her Heavenly Father and seek the wisdom He promised to those who asked.

৯

Bone weary, Lucas could barely keep his eyes open long enough to strip off his outer clothes and hit the sack. He hadn't formulated an actual prayer of thanks when he'd heard Chesapeake's return, but a steady stream of wordless praise had more than expressed his deepest feelings, and he didn't feel he could improve on that. The animal could have fared far worse. Noah, however, he would deal with later.

His mind went over the evening's events beginning with Rosemary's arrival, and he smiled. Melinda and Amy hadn't been the only ones who'd been surprised by the golden-haired milliner's unexpected visit. She had been a staunch friend to him since Francie's passing. Never pushy or intrusive but always available in the background whenever he needed to talk or have some sewing done. And she had a pleasant nature. For someone who had hinted strongly that she wasn't ready to tackle child-rearing, she sure had gone to considerable trouble making those new dresses for Melinda and Amy. The girls had been thrilled.

Too bad Amy had to have that accident. A woman accustomed to being around youngsters wouldn't have been put off in the least by a little spilled milk. But obviously to someone like Rosemary, it was a catastrophe. Probably in time she would get over the tendency to think that way.

Would she welcome the chance? Lucas wondered. *Was this the reason she'd come all the way out here today—just to let me know she's open to the suggestion?*

He'd never been really sure that Rosemary liked his daughters. She did try to converse with them—tried real hard—but somehow it didn't come off natural-like.

With Annora, things were different. From the first day she set foot on the farm, she took the girls right into her heart. . . and the reverse was equally true. Annora just fit in. Fit in fine.

Recollecting her genuine concern for Chesapeake, her willingness to help in whatever way she could, Lucas realized how he was coming to depend on her. The two of them hadn't started out on the right foot, exactly, and Lucas had to admit he had taken advantage of her in the beginning—mostly in the hope of driving her away. But now, she was such a part of the place he could barely picture the farm without her there.

In fact, Lucas wasn't sure he wanted to. With an involuntary yawn, he turned over.

❧

Lucas was in the middle of his chores the next morning when he sensed someone's presence in the barn. He turned.

"Leave it to old Ches to get home all right," Noah said nonchalantly, sauntering toward the end stall, his hands in his pockets.

The sight of that cocky smirk sent a surge of white heat through Lucas, exploding the rage inside him. "Yep," he replied offhandedly, as if they were discussing the weather. "Thanks to you, he *limped* back a few hours later!" The handle of the rake banged to the floor as Lucas lunged at his brother, slamming him against the boards of the next stall.

Noah landed on the floor. Winded, surprised, he lumbered to his feet.

The second he was upright, Lucas lit into him again. "This is for Ches," he said with a hard punch to the gut, "and this is for Annora." His knuckles connected with Noah's jaw, knocking him to the dirt. Hard. Blood trickled from the corner of his mouth. The sight of it gave Lucas a perverse sort of satisfaction. He'd wanted to catch the kid off his guard, make him feel some of the shock Annora had experienced. For some reason that was very important.

Noah's own anger came to the fore. He scrambled up, fists raised in front of him. "You always were an overbearing lout," he hissed, "thinkin' you're better 'n everybody else." He jabbed at Lucas.

The blow caught Lucas in the eye. Stumbling backward a step, he regained his balance. "Better that than a good-for-nothing, lazy—" His words were cut off when Noah threw himself at him. They crashed to the ground again in a flurry of punches and grunts, rolling over and over in the dust.

The patter of small feet sounded above the melee. "Pa! Uncle Noah!"

Lucas jerked up his head and caught Melinda and Amy gawking in horrified shock. Then the two of them burst into tears.

⚬

Annora was busy getting breakfast when she heard a commotion from the barn. Glancing in that direction, she saw Amy coming at a dead run, screaming. She dropped what she was doing and flew to the door, her arms outstretched to the little girl. "What is it?"

"Miss Annora!" the child cried, flinging her arms about Annora's waist. "They're fightin'! Pa and Uncle Noah. And Sissy's cryin'. I'm afraid!"

"Oh, dear!" Annora hugged her tight.

"They. . .they're hittin'! Punchin'!" the child sobbed. "Like they don't ev–even l–love each other anymore."

Knowing how upsetting the small scuffle she'd witnessed

outside the lean-to had seemed, Annora could think only of Melinda—and of sparing her from further distress or possibly even hurt. Taking Amy's hand, she drew her to the sofa. "You sit here, sweetheart. I'll go get Sissy. Everything will be all right." But inside her heart, she had more than a few doubts.

On winged feet, she ran to the barn, where she found the men still at it, arms and legs flailing amid thuds and grunts. Moving immediately to Melinda, who cowered in a corner with her hands covering her face, Annora swept the child up into her arms. The thought that two grown men would carry on with apparently no concern for how their conduct might affect innocent children made Annora furious.

"Would you look at yourselves!" she hollered. "Carrying on like common ruffians—and in front of babies, yet! It's the most disgraceful, despicable thing I have ever seen in my life!" Branding the pair with every ounce of scorn she possessed, she stomped toward the exit but turned around in the doorway. "And don't you dare come to my table with blood and dirt all over you. *Either of you!*" And with that, she flounced away.

By the time she reached the house, she cringed, remembering the remarks she had so rashly blurted out in the barn. But the fact was, her only concern had been six-year-old Melinda.

Once in the sanctity of the home, both girls began to calm down.

"Why did our Pa fight with Uncle Noah?" Amy asked.

Wrapping an arm around each of them, Annora formulated her reply. "I suppose even grown-ups get mad sometimes, when things hurt them very badly inside. But when it's all over, they kind of forget about what bothered them, and then things go back the way they were before."

"Promise?"

"I promise. Now, let's wash those tears away. There are two men who are sure to be pretty hungry by the time breakfast is ready." But the truth was, her own confident words rang hollow as she sliced off more bacon and broke some extra eggs into the bowl.

Sure enough, though, when Annora clanged the metal triangle a short while later to signal breakfast, she saw Lucas trudging toward the house. Not too many yards behind him, Noah followed. A short stop at the barrel to scrub up and comb their hair, and they tramped into the kitchen.

Melinda and Amy, their eyes huge as saucers, snuggled a trifle closer to each other in mute silence as their subdued father and equally collected uncle pulled out a couple of chairs.

Annora, trying to act as if it were the most natural thing in the world to show up for breakfast bruised, with black eyes and bloodied noses, quickly bowed her head. "Dear Father, we thank You for this new day and for Your goodness to us. Please bless this food to our bodies and us to Your service. Amen."

The heavy silence that followed only magnified every crunch of crisp bacon and every swallow. Feeling more than ever responsible for the great chasm that had torn the two brothers apart, the tension underscored Annora's conviction that, regardless of Lucas's decision, she would not stay on at the Brent farm.

She would pack her things today. And at the first possible opportunity, she would ask Lucas to drive her to town.

seventeen

After cleaning up the breakfast clutter, Annora made certain the girls were occupied before going in search of Lucas. She found him alone in the barn, kneeling as he undid the wrap on Chesapeake's injury.

"How's the leg doing this morning?" she asked, squelching a wince at the sight of her employer's shiner and swollen knuckles. Not a word had been said regarding the confrontation between him and Noah, and she was not about to pry into the matter, even though she suspected it had partly concerned her.

"Quite an improvement over last night," he said evenly, but he did not meet her gaze as he applied a fresh dressing and bound it with a clean bandage.

Now that she was here, Annora was at a loss about how to approach the subject uppermost in her mind. She pretended intense engrossment in observing Lucas at work until he picked up on her silence.

"Was there something you wanted?" he finally asked.

"Yes, actually." She nibbled the inside corner of her lip momentarily, then pressed on. "My trial month is about up."

He nodded as he kept working. "And I suppose you're wondering if you still have a job."

"No, not. . .exactly. I've decided to. . .seek employment elsewhere."

He stopped his ministrations and stood to his feet, eyeing her with that piercing gaze she had once considered annoying. Now it seemed different somehow. Challenging. Unnerving. And with Lucas towering over her, Annora felt more vulnerable. It was all she could do to ignore the jittering that started up in her stomach and slowly made its way down to her knees. She knew that if she dared look into his eyes for more than a second or two, he'd discover the depth of her true feelings.

"That's why I've come to speak to you," she blurted before she changed her mind. "I would like someone to drive me into town later today so I can make other arrangements." She ventured moving her gaze upward from his middle shirt button so she could make out his expression.

"This is what you want?" he asked, narrowing his eyes as if reading her thoughts.

Annora's first impulse was to say no, but honesty was the last thing she could afford right now. Even if she were positive it was natural for brothers to come to blows occasionally—and she couldn't imagine such a thing—just knowing she had been the cause of the rift in this family was unforgivable. It must never happen again. "It's what I've decided. I do believe the implied agreement was that either of us could nullify the arrangement."

"That's news to me. But if it's what you want, I'll see that you get there."

His swift acquiescence caught her off guard. What had she been hoping for—his flat refusal? An argument, at least? She gave herself a mental shake. "Thank you. I'll go and start packing."

He gave a noncommittal nod and resumed his earlier task.

But as she turned and walked away, Annora felt a marked change in the atmosphere, and she was aware of his eyes staring after her. She couldn't afford to dwell on what he must be thinking of her. . .not when so much of her concentration was being used just to keep her legs going.

Informing Melinda and Amy of her decision was even harder. The pair spied her through her open doorway in mid-afternoon, after Annora lugged her trunk atop her cot and began filling it with her belongings.

The hoop Melinda had been rolling fell to the ground, and she charged into the lean-to, her little sister a mere step behind. "Hey! What are you doin', Miss Annora?"

"I. . .um, have to go away."

"You mean, to visit somebody?" Amy wanted to know.

Annora shook her head and continued folding garments and stacking them in neat piles. "No. I mean, I'm leaving and going someplace else."

"But–but–" Even as the six-year-old's eyes swam with tears, she swiped them away in anger, her lower lip quivering. "I thought you loved us."

"I do, sweetheart. I love both of you very, very much."

"Then why are you leavin'?" she insisted.

"Who will take care of us?" Amy whimpered.

Knowing she should not have expected to escape easily from this heart-stopping pair, Annora sighed and quit packing. She gathered the girls into her arms and sat down on the foot of her bed with one youngster on either side of her. "When I first came here, it was only for a short time. You know, a trial. None of us expected it to be forever. Well, now my time is up, so I'll be moving on. Your pa will take care of you again, he and your uncle Noah. And you've both become such good helpers, I'm sure that with all four of you working together, you won't have a problem keeping everything looking clean and nice. You'll see."

Amy turned her eyes up to Annora. "But we don't want you to go away—like our mama. We want you to stay and live here with us."

"Well, we can't always have things the way we want them," Annora began.

"You mean, you don't want to stay," Melinda accused, her eyes brimming again.

"No, that is not what I mean," Annora said gently, brushing some stray dark hairs out of the child's face. "The fact is, the time has come for me to do what's right. For everyone."

Melinda hiked her chin. "It doesn't seem right to me. Or fair, either. Not when we need you."

"I'm truly sorry you feel that way, sweetheart," Annora said softly, "but I'm afraid this is how it must be."

"Then. . .then. . .just. . .go!" Melinda railed between clenched teeth as she sprang to her feet. "You don't love us, and. . .and. . .I wish you never ever came here!" And with that, she bolted from the room in tears.

Amy didn't say a word. She stared reproachfully up at Annora for a few seconds before going rigid and pulling free. Then she stomped out of the lean-to with one scathing glance backward.

Yes, I do love you, my darlings, Annora's heart called after them in silence. *But you're not the only ones I love. . .and that is the problem.* Her own eyes smarted, but she determinedly blinked back the tears. Hard as it was to deal with the way Lucas's daughters were hurting, maybe it was all for the best. They had gone somewhere by themselves to sulk. They were angry now—and perhaps feeling somewhat betrayed—but eventually they would get over it. At least she wouldn't have to tear herself away from two little girls who were sobbing their hearts out in a wrenching scene she'd never be able to erase from her memory.

She had not been packed for long before Lucas rapped at her door. "The wagon's hitched up. So whenever you're ready—"

"I'm ready now," Annora replied, amazed that her voice had not wavered. She opened the door and motioned toward her trunk and valise, then watched as her employer effortlessly hefted the ungainly travel chest to his shoulder. She donned the bonnet that matched her green traveling ensemble and followed him to the wagon, the handle of her valise held in both hands.

After Lucas situated the luggage in the wagon bed and handed her up to the seat, Annora searched everywhere for a glimpse of Melinda or Amy, but they were nowhere to be seen. She tried not to let it bother her that the girls were cheating her out of the chance to wave good-bye, to reassure them that things would turn out all right in the end.

Drawing a stabilizing breath, she relaxed her shoulders and composed herself for departure from the place that had spared her a life of unhappiness back in Philadelphia. Odd, how on the day she had arrived, she had begged Lucas not to make her leave. . .but now, she couldn't stay even if he asked her to. Fighting tears, she shoved the unwelcome thoughts forcefully from her mind. She would have ample time later for wallowing in self-pity.

The silence cloaking the drive to Cheyenne was almost unbearable. From the corner of her eye, Annora observed Lucas's stiff posture. His face was completely blank—and he had yet to say a word.

That lasted the entire route.

When they finally came within sight of the town, Annora felt a measure of relief—which quickly faded when Lucas pulled up to the railroad station and stopped.

"What are you doing?"

"Buying your fare back East." He hopped down and went for her baggage.

"But I don't want to go there," she countered, climbing down on her own. "I haven't enough funds."

"Yes, you have. I was supposed to pay your traveling expenses, if you recall. One direction or both, makes no difference to me."

"But that's absurd. I really don't—"

He paid her no mind but strode to the ticket window. "The young lady would like to travel to Philadelphia. When's the next train thereabouts?" he asked the clerk.

"Can't get that far east right now," the man answered, peering over his spectacles. "Bad rains in Ohio. Washed out part of the track bed."

"Well, how long till it's fixed?" Lucas groused.

"Couple weeks, a month—can't say for sure."

Having overheard the exchange from directly behind Lucas, Annora breathed a sigh of relief. Perhaps he'd listen to reason now. "I planned to stay at the hotel while I seek another position," she announced.

"Makes more sense for you to come back to the farm while you wait. Then if you're still set on leaving a couple weeks from now, I won't stop you."

"Lucas, please." In an effort to keep from tapping her foot in impatience, Annora filled her lungs and then let all the breath out at once. "I'm trying to tell you, it is impossible for me to go back to Philadelphia. There's no place for me there. Just book me a room at the hotel for now and let me make my own way. Please."

He frowned and searched her face.

"Please," she repeated.

"Why does it have to be now, this minute? Can you tell me that?"

"No, I cannot."

"If it's Noah you're leery of. . ."

Annora shook her head emphatically. "This is just something I have to do. I put in the trial month we agreed upon, and now that it's over, there's no reason for me to stay. I. . . want to do something different. Something someplace else."

"It doesn't make sense, Annora. I thought you were happy with. . .with us. What am I supposed to tell the girls when I get back home and you're not with me?"

"I've already spoken to Melinda and Amy, and we said our good-byes. They'll be fine, in time."

He shook his head. But when he opened his mouth as if to speak, no comment emerged. With a sidelong glare, he retrieved her trunk and carried it back to the wagon, then drove her to the hotel. Within a half-hour, he secured a room and brought her baggage upstairs.

"Well," he said flatly, "I guess this is it."

"Yes." She feigned the brightest smile she could muster and tossed her bonnet onto the bed. "Thank you for carrying my things up for me."

His hat in his hands, he turned it around and around while he stood there in the doorway, looking for all the world as if he had something to say. Only he said nothing.

"I. . .appreciate your giving me that chance I asked for, Lucas," Annora finally remarked. "It was rather an. . .adventure, getting to know you and your darling girls."

". . .who are gonna be miserable without you around," he finished, his gaze a challenge, his expression unfathomable for an uncomfortable moment or more. "Look," he said with a huff, "if you're gonna be here for awhile, would it be all right if I bring the girls to visit now and then?"

Annora wanted that more than anything, but she knew it would only prolong their sadness. Better to make a quick break and let them get on with their lives. She swallowed and shook her head. "It's best if they let go now," she said softly.

He gave a perfunctory nod. "As you wish. Oh." He reached into the inside pocket of his vest. "Here's the rest of the money I owe for your travel, or whatever. . ."

"That's not necessary, Lucas."

"Horsefeathers, Annora!" he exclaimed. "You worked for me. Worked hard. I owe you something for that, and besides, you don't know when you'll find another job. You might need this."

She could not fault his reasoning. But neither could she bear his presence much longer without falling apart. With all her resolve, she held out her hand.

Lucas pressed the roll of bills into her palm and closed her fingers around it. When he did not let go right away, her gaze was drawn to his. "Seems hardly sufficient just to say thanks for everything."

She moistened her lips, noting the pain in his eyes, wondering if it resulted from more than just the swollen discoloration around one of them. "I was just doing my job," she said lightly, hating the high pitch of her voice yet amazed she could utter anything at all with him holding her hand in both of his and staring into her very heart and soul.

His eyes slowly roved her face, finally settling on her lips. Annora's heart refused to beat for an eternal moment.

"Well, take care of yourself, y'hear?" he said softly.

"Y–you, too," she whispered, starting to tremble inside.

With a nod and a half-smile, Lucas released his grip, then left, closing the door behind him.

Annora tried not to watch him drive away. But despite her best intentions, she gravitated to the window before he was even outside. And then the sight of him leaving town was obscured by a veil of tears.

eighteen

Annora sat up in her bed at the hotel and struggled to breathe through her stuffy nose. She felt empty. Wasted. She had not wept so hard since the loss of her parents—but then, nothing else in her life had hurt so deeply. . .until now. Her eyes burned, her head ached—aggravated even more by the raucous tinkle of piano music from a few doors down the street, to say nothing of the loud voices coming from everywhere.

She could not permit her thoughts to drift to the Brent farm, to children who in all likelihood had cried themselves to sleep, or to the dark-haired farmer with the gentle blue eyes who had managed to snag her heart in the short while she had known him. Every time she gave in to those memories, a new rush of tears followed.

Having turned to God's Word for the comfort that always sustained her through dark times, Annora was dismayed that her watery eyes couldn't focus on the words. In despair, she hugged the worn book to her breast and rocked back and forth, imagining the mental picture her father had always painted for her of being held in the arms of God. Somehow that helped. But she had a strong suspicion that pain this intense would take a long, long time to get over.

Just as she expected, the next morning, the mirror above the washstand revealed the unmistakable marks the endless night had left on her puffy face. Her swollen eyes were rimmed with pink and underscored by dark circles. But like it or not, she had to go on, make plans for her future, however bleak it seemed. She poured cool water from the pitcher into the bowl, washed and changed into a fresh day gown of rust linen, then went downstairs for some coffee.

"Morning, miss," the bookish clerk, Jenson Samuels, called from the lobby desk as Annora descended the staircase. "Breakfast is being served in the dining room, if you're interested." He indicated a set of open double doors leading from the main hallway.

"Thank you." A polite smile was about all Annora could come up with as she followed his directions.

Even eyes as tired as her own could not help but appreciate the finely laid out accouterments of the spacious room—its rich Oriental carpet and an abundance of matching wooden tables in varied sizes. She surmised that at the evening's supper hour, with the ornate gasoliers casting a warm glow over the crisp white linens and best china, it must be truly lovely.

Nodding as she passed the only other occupants, an elderly couple occupying a table in the center of the room, Annora chose a small square one for herself near a window while she waited to be served.

By midmorning, Annora was feeling more like herself. After her time of Bible reading and prayer, she threw her light shawl about her shoulders and walked the short distance to the church where she'd attended service with Lucas and his daughters. The sight assailed her with memories she could not bear to dwell on, but she hiked her chin and strode purposely up the steps, hoping to find it unlocked for meditation.

Thankfully, it was. The door squeaked open on its hinges, and she stepped inside.

"May I help you, miss?" the moon-faced pastor said as he strode toward her from the sanctuary. "Oh. . .Miss Nolan, as I recall."

"Yes, thank you for remembering me, Reverend Gardner," Annora answered, appreciating the kindness in the man's smile and bearing.

"What brings you by today, lass? A problem out at the farm? Some needed counsel?"

"Well, actually, I came by to check your public board. I

was hoping to apply for a new position here in town."

Obviously puzzled, he ran gnarled fingers through his thinning hair. "You're no longer employed by Lucas Brent?"

Annora smiled and shook her head. "No, that was only temporary. I'm looking for something permanent now."

"Well. Hmm. I'm afraid I cannot think of anything suitable among the present notices. You're more than welcome to look for yourself, of course." He motioned toward the cluttered board on the opposite side of the vestibule.

Her heart sinking, Annora stepped toward it, scanning the raft of bulletins pinned every which way before her eyes. All of them seemed to pertain to men. Trail guides, surveyors, ranch hands, railroad workers. . .She exhaled a disappointed breath and turned to leave.

"Wait a minute," the minister said, rubbing his chin in thought.

Annora stopped.

"Seems a member of my flock did mention something the other day—the manager of the Inter-Ocean Hotel. One of his chambermaids became ill a week or so ago, and he was decrying how shorthanded they are. If you could, perchance, fill in until their regular girl recovers, maybe a position more to your liking might open up for you. Would that be of interest?"

"It surely would," Annora replied, feeling hopeful at last. "I happen to be staying there. I'll go see about it at once. Thank you ever so much!" Resisting the ridiculous urge to kiss the man of the cloth, she bobbed in a quick curtsy instead.

"And since you're residing within such close proximity to the church," he added, a twinkle in his eye, "might I expect to see your bright face among the flock next Lord's Day?"

"You just might. Thanks again, Reverend." With a new spring in her step, Annora took her leave. But before she'd gone half the distance to the hotel, she envisioned herself walking into the sanctuary on any given Sunday and seeing Lucas and the girls. . .seated, no doubt, with a gloating

Rosemary Evans. And her spirit crashed to the ground.

"Well, well," came the milliner's voice from the doorway of her shop, as if Annora's thoughts had caused the woman to materialize. "Shopping again so soon?"

Annora's mind had been so occupied with her own matters, she had forgotten to walk on the opposite side of the street, where she'd have been less noticeable. "Miss Evans." She dipped her bonneted head in a respectful greeting.

The elegantly clad woman's hazel eyes swept the street in both directions, likely searching for Lucas and his daughters. "Where is everyone?" Rosemary asked.

"At home," Annora said evasively. "I'm on errands of my own."

"How. . .interesting."

"Yes. Well, I'm afraid I'm in a bit of a hurry just now. Do have a pleasant day, won't you?"

"Indeed."

Before further comments could be drawn from Annora, she hastened on. It galled her that Rosemary knew she was in Cheyenne, for in all likelihood the woman would go out of her way to ascertain the reason for her being there. But she'd have found out soon enough anyway, since Sunday was just around the corner. With a sigh, Annora ducked into the mercantile and browsed briefly through the merchandise. Then she inquired about a rear door, and with a sigh of relief, took the roundabout way to the Inter-Ocean Hotel, where she promptly applied for the job.

To her amazement, a delighted Mr. Samuels insisted she be given a thorough tour of the facility, introduced to the staff, and put to work at once.

So began a new phase of her life.

Once again, Annora appreciated her background. Keeping fresh sheets on the beds of a huge three-story hotel and tidying the scores of sleeping chambers kept her occupied from early morning until quite late in the afternoon. And on particularly busy occasions, she was also prevailed upon to help during evening mealtime as well. Weary and exhausted, she now fell asleep the instant her head touched her pillow—regardless of the town noise. But since her job was only temporary, at least she was not asked to relocate to the servants' quarters.

The unending toil kept her too busy to think, let alone differentiate one day from another. . .so the sight of Lucas Brent's wagon rumbling past the hotel several mornings later was most unexpected. Caught by surprise, she paused in her dusting. He, Noah, and the girls were decked out in their Sunday best.

They must be on their way to church. Annora pressed closer to the window, watching after them. Part of her rejoiced to see the Brent family united again, but another part of her had to battle the urge to open the floodgates of her heart. . .to the tears never far from the surface during her waking hours.

She sighed and resumed her duties with considerably less enthusiasm.

Awhile later, as she swept the front steps, her heart sank to see Lucas drive by again. . .this time with a very animated Rosemary perched between him and Noah on the wide seat. Melinda and Amy now carried new dolls, obviously storebought. The sight of the little ones made Annora's eyes sting.

Endeavoring not to draw attention to herself with any quick movements, she continued sweeping. But Lucas's wordless glance found her. Her heart lurched within her breast as she gave him a tiny smile and went back to the chore, determined to resist the persistent moisture in her eyes that made her turn her back to the street.

That night in the dark solitude of her chamber, she finally gave in to what she hoped would be her last fit of weeping. After all, her prayers had been answered, hadn't they? Lucas and Noah had repaired their broken relationship, the girls appeared fine. Perhaps, she told herself, they would find themselves in a complete family circle once again. . .even if it was with Rosemary as their stepmother. That was the hardest of all to swallow, but Annora prayed that God would help her to accept it.

Knowing she wouldn't be able to sleep anytime soon, she went to her trunk and removed two sheets of writing stationery. Tonight she would pour out her heartaches to Lesley.

ॐ

Lucas closed the storybook and ruffled Amy's hair. " 'Night, pumpkin. You, too, my other pumpkin," he said, reaching to stroke Melinda's soft cheek.

" 'Night, Pa," they both said, their unhappy little smiles tearing at his insides. Hardly a day had passed that they hadn't brought Annora's name into a dozen conversations. He was just thankful they hadn't spied her earlier that morning as they passed the hotel. Bad enough that his own pulse kicked up in that crazy way at the sight of her. He could almost picture the girls jumping over the side of the wagon bed and running to hug her. Then afterward, they'd have been inconsolable, knowing that, no, she would not be coming out even to visit, and yes, they would have to do without her forever.

He'd detected particular unease in his older daughter today. She had been uncharacteristically quiet, and just as he rose from their bedside chair, Melinda turned her troubled face to his. "Pa?"

"Yes, honey-girl?"

"Is Miss Rosemary gonna be our new mama?"

He slowly filled his lungs, then exhaled in a ragged breath. "Would you like that?"

She merely shrugged.

"I like my new dolly," Amy chimed in. "Miss Rosemary buys us pretty things. She says she wants to be our friend."

"But she's. . ." Melinda's eyes suddenly brimmed and a tear rolled down the side of her face and into her hair. "She's not Annora," she wailed, her voice catching on a sob.

"Hey, pumpkin," he said in his most soothing tone, "I know you've been kind of sad since Annora went away."

"Be–because. . .I. . .m–made her g–go."

As his daughter's tears swiftly became a deluge, Lucas bent over to pat her shoulder in what seemed to him a hopelessly inadequate attempt to administer comfort. But her words disturbed him greatly. "What do you mean?"

The six-year-old sniffed and rubbed at her wet cheeks, smearing traces of dirt into uneven smudges. "When she s–said she couldn't stay, I–I told her to g–go away," she admitted in a tiny voice. "And that. . .I wished she–she'd. . .never. . . come!" Almost hysterical now, she rolled over and sobbed into her pillow, in heart-wrenching gasps that shook her tiny frame.

When the worst began to subside, Lucas picked her up and lowered himself to the mattress, hugging her hard. "Well, I'm sure you didn't mean it, pumpkin, and Annora knew in her heart that you didn't, too. The fact that she had to leave was not your fault."

"Truly?" she whimpered.

"Truly. And everything is gonna be all right. You'll see." But even as he felt her relax, he wondered how and when that would ever be true.

જ

Annora navigated the dining room, filling water glasses for the unusually large assemblage of patrons and seeing to their various needs.

"Excuse me, miss," a portly gentleman with thick side whiskers said, waving to her from where he was seated with a group of four. "Would you mind checking on our order? We've been waiting for some time."

"Yes, of course. I'll be but a moment." Nodding, she spun on her heel and started for the kitchen.

"Why, Annora Nolan!" cried a familiar feminine voice. "How absolutely lovely to see you!"

Recognizing Hope Johnston's smiling face as she rose from a table of uniformed men and their female companions,

Annora gasped at the sight of her traveling mate from the train. She stepped into a huge hug. "And you!" she finally managed. "This is certainly a surprise."

"Yes, is it not?" Reclaiming her seat, the slender young military wife gestured to the tall and fair-complexioned man in blue next to her. "Phillip, you remember my mentioning the sweet friend I made during my journey. I'd like you to meet Annora Nolan. Annora, this is my husband, Lieutenant Phillip Johnston."

"Lieutenant," she said with a nod as he rose to take the hand she offered. "I'm very pleased to meet you."

"Oh, miss-s-s-s," the heavyset man across the way reminded her pointedly.

Turning back to Hope, she winced in embarrassment. "I don't mean to be rude, but I'm on duty just now."

"Of course. But is there any chance we might have a word before I must go?" the delicate-featured woman asked.

"Perhaps, if things slow down." And with that, Annora hurried away.

Half an hour later, she spotted the group from Fort Russell as they left their table and began walking toward the lobby. Checking to make certain she wasn't needed, she hurried to Hope's side and slipped an arm about her. "I'm sorry I wasn't able to visit with you. We've so much to catch up on. How's sweet Rachel? And you? How've you been?"

"Fine, fine, couldn't be better. But I thought you were contracted to work for a local farmer. Housekeeper, wasn't it?"

"Yes, and I did. But my trial period ended, and I. . .decided to move on. I'm working here temporarily now, filling in for a girl who's ill."

"Oh. Well, how providential that our paths would cross again. As it happens, a dear friend of ours at the fort, the colonel's wife, recently suffered a mild stroke and is in dire need of a live-in companion and housekeeper. Not the most glamorous of pastimes, I'll allow—but it would provide an opportunity for us to renew our friendship. If you think you might want the job, contact me through the postmaster as soon as possible."

"I will. Thanks for telling me about it." With one last hug, Annora reluctantly relinquished her hold. "Take care, Hope."

"I will. And I do hope you apply for that position."

"I'll pray about it. Truth is, it might be exactly what I need right now."

Yes, she affirmed mentally. She knew very well what her heart needed—wanted. But sitting here in Cheyenne when that possibility was utterly hopeless. . .Besides, how many more times could she bear the sight of that wagon rolling by?

No, I'll work on that letter. Tonight.

nineteen

The more Annora prayed about applying for the position at Fort Russell, the greater became the sense of peace that enveloped her. Staying on indefinitely in Cheyenne, where she'd run into Lucas Brent from time to time, would be like applying iodine to a brushburn. No, it was time to move on, give the empty chasm inside her a chance to fill with new friends, new faces.

She could not imagine any man ever measuring up to the standard her heart now required, thanks to that lonely widower from Cheyenne. She would compare every single one to him for the rest of her life. But in time, perhaps a love would come along that was almost as precious as this ill-fated one.

There was no sense in letting circumstances get her down, Annora decided. Nor was there any point in waiting for the hotel manager to inform her of the exact day when the regular chambermaid would report for duty. The sooner she posted the message to Hope Johnston expressing a willingness to become live-in companion to the colonel's bedridden wife, the sooner her shattered heart would mend. During her noon break, she would mail the letter she had written last evening.

Her mind settled, Annora changed into a full-sleeved shirtwaist, indigo skirt, and long bib apron for work. She tied a red kerchief over her hair and reported to the supply room for the clean linens the morning would require.

Jenson Samuels was waiting for her when she arrived. "Oh. Miss Nolan," he said, twisting a pen nervously in his fingers, his bespectacled gaze never quite meeting hers. "I wanted you to know we've been most appreciative of the quality of your work."

"Why, thank you, Mr. Samuels. The job was a godsend to me."

"Yes." He cleared his throat. "And it was very good of you to fill in for our Sadie. But she has recovered sufficiently to return to her duties, so I've been given the unpleasant task of informing you that after today, your services will no longer be needed. I'm sorry."

"Oh, please, don't be. I've been offered another position," Annora assured him, "and I'd already made up my mind to accept it the moment my job ends here. So I'm not in the least put out by Sadie's return."

"Well," he said, considerably more at ease. "That is welcome news. However, should you ever need employment in the future, please let us be the first to know. Your dependability and fine service have earned our highest recommendation."

"Thank you, sir. I appreciate those kind words. And I just might do that someday." Smiling, she opened the supply room door and began filling her arms with clean white sheets.

The man lingered uncertainly for another second or two before handing her a list of rooms needing her attention. Then, with a cursory nod, he left for his station in the lobby.

This being her final day as chambermaid, Annora breezed through the entire morning, returning to her room slightly after noon. She freshened up and changed into a clean dress, then unpinned her chignon and brushed her long waves, fastening the sides back with ivory combs. All the while she worked, she had thought of the letter she'd composed and how it needed to be delivered to the postmaster.

She made a mental note to do that when she finished packing most of her belongings, omitting only what would be needed for another day or two. Crossing to her trunk, Annora opened the heavy lid.

Light from the window slanted across the paper lining of the chest, and for the first time, Annora noticed a peculiar unevenness in the bottom—as if a small portion had been cut to make a hidden compartment, one all but invisible against the liner's printed design. She frowned and knelt to pry at the edge with a fingernail. It popped open, and she raised the flap.

"Mama's jewelry!" she gasped, too amazed to do anything but gape at the pieces she'd asked Lesley to sell for her. Plucking the familiar items from the velvet lining the compartment, Annora saw a folded note and recognized the young woman's distinctive stationery. Her eyes misted as she opened it.

Dearest Nora,

One day you will find this tiny hiding place, and when you do, I hope it will brighten your day. Knowing how very much your mother's treasures meant to you, neither Michael nor I could bear to sell or pawn them. Both of us had been putting away a little money toward the day when we might wed. The decision to purchase your fare as our parting gift was mutual as well as joyous. We will always consider you as dear to us as a sister. May the Lord keep His loving hand upon you always and grant you every happiness.

With deepest love,
Lesley

Annora stared through her tears at her best friend's precise penmanship. She might have guessed those two would concoct such a loving tribute to the relationship they had shared in Philadelphia. If she lived to be a hundred, she doubted she would ever again find friends so close and dear.

Pressing her late mother's possessions to her heart for a few breathless seconds, Annora replaced them inside the secret compartment, then dried her cheeks and went to gather clothes from the armoire.

A knock on the door interrupted the task before the trunk was half full. When she answered the summons, her heart skipped a beat.

"Lucas!"

In a jacket and work clothes, with his hair slicked back and his hat in his hands, he flashed a sheepish, one-sided smile. "May I come in?"

"Of–of course," she whispered. She stood aside while he entered, leaving the door ajar behind him. Annora schooled herself not to stare. She could not afford to let his presence affect her, not after the limited ground she had gained over her despondency. "Is something the matter?" she managed past a huge lump in her throat. "The girls—they're all right?"

A nod.

"Chesapeake, then. Is he doing well?"

Another nod. "He's starting to show some interest in those pretty little mares that have been admiring him from afar up until now," he said lightly. Then his expression turned sober. "Actually, I came to make sure that *you're* well. You looked kind of. . .tired the other day."

"I probably was," she confessed, extremely relieved to hear that nothing was wrong with either Melinda or Amy. "I'd put in a few rather long days here, filling in for an absent chambermaid."

"Ah."

"It's. . .kind of you to be concerned, though," Annora said. She had almost used the word *sweet* but caught herself just in time. He'd think she was a dolt. *And he's merely your former employer, remember*, she cautioned herself. *Don't make more of this than it is.*

His gaze, which had casually roamed over Annora from head to toe before coming to rest on her face, now meandered about the room. It halted on the partially packed trunk. His dark brows flared. "Packing?"

"Yes. I've taken another job. Well, that is, I've been offered one and agreed tentatively. I'm just about to post my formal acceptance."

"In town?"

She shook her head. The temptation to elaborate on its being a mere three miles away at Fort Russell was almost too strong to resist. Everything within her wanted to let him know she'd still be near enough to visit, to keep in touch—but she clamped her lips together.

"I see." Moving deeper into the room, Lucas surveyed the neatly folded clothes occupying the bed and the trunk, sized up the simple furnishings and the view from the window, where he stood gazing outside without a word.

Annora had the impression there was more to his coming here than he'd related, and watching him idly strolling around her chamber somehow reinforced the notion. But he'd either tell her or he wouldn't, it was entirely up to him. Meanwhile, she repressed her growing jitters.

"Well," he finally said, expelling a whoosh of air. "You obviously have things to do. I shouldn't keep you. Wouldn't want you to. . .miss your train."

She knew he was fishing for information, but she wasn't about to give him any. Best to make the break quick. Clean.

"I'm glad to see you're all right," Lucas said again. "Real glad."

Annora gave him a polite nod. Maintaining her composure was using up every ounce of her strength. If he didn't leave soon, her nerves were going to fray completely. *Please go, Lucas. Go, before I say something really dumb.*

He focused his attention on her again, and his shoulders flattened in resignation. Three strides brought him back to where she remained rooted to the floor. "I guess this is good-bye, then."

"I guess," she murmured, wise enough not to trust her voice.

"For good."

She nodded.

"In that case, I. . .wish you well." He continued to stare, his enigmatic expression gradually turning to one of acceptance.

"I'll never forget you, Annora."

"Nor I you." Raising her lashes, she allowed herself one more searching look at those dusky blue eyes of his. . . . It would have to do for the rest of her life. Only with the greatest reluctance did she finally break eye contact. "Good-bye, Lucas," she whispered, offering her hand.

His fingers closed around it, but instead of giving a mere handshake, he raised it to his lips and brushed a feather-light kiss to her skin. Then, hesitating but an instant, he left, shutting the door after himself.

The back of Annora's hand burned with his kiss, and she pressed it to her lips as her heart contracted with exquisite pain. She tried not to listen to him stride down the hall. Then the stairs.

Placing a palm over her pounding heart in a futile attempt to restore its more normal pace, she closed her eyes. *At least that was our final good-bye*, she thought consolingly. *I could never endure another.*

A dull ache filled her as she made her way to the window. The sight of Lucas's departure would likely be the final glimpse of him she would have in her lifetime. . . . And she was helpless against the need to fill her eyes with him one last time.

&

Where are you going? Lucas's conscience railed before he'd made it halfway downstairs. *You already lost one love. Let this one slip through your fingers, and you're a blithering idiot!* He halted so suddenly, a fellow descending a step behind crashed into him. "Sorry," Lucas mumbled and moved aside to allow the man to pass.

But she has another job. Plans. He mulled over what Annora had said, trying to recollect her exact words. *Agreed tentatively*, wasn't that it? *About to* post her formal acceptance. Which means. . .she hasn't exactly committed. In the darkness of his heart, that spark of hope was almost blinding in its brilliance. A slow smile emerged.

Could be the lamest thing I've ever set out to do. "But I'm still gonna try," he said under his breath. He retraced his steps to her room. Removing his Stetson, he raked his fingers through his hair. Swallowed. Drew a strengthening breath. Rapped.

The look on her face was absolutely priceless when the door opened. "Lucas!" A pause. "Did you. . .forget something?"

"As a matter of fact, I did. May I come in?"

Obviously confused, she backed away. "What is it?"

"You, uh, still owe me two days," he blurted, saying the first thing that came to his mind.

"What?" Her cheeks pinkened. . .a shade he quite liked.

"Our agreement, remember? For a month. Well, according to my calculations, you left two days early." Smug over the absurdly flimsy straw he'd grasped, his internal grin widened into a broad smile. "I want you to come finish out your time."

"Don't be ridiculous," Annora said in that plucky way he had grown to love. She crossed her arms.

Lucas conceded that Miss Annora Nolan was not one who could be coerced. Only complete sincerity would cut through the reserve she wrapped around herself like a feather quilt. He dispensed with the humor and took her hand in both of his, gripping all the tighter at her subtle attempt to tug free. "Look, Annora," he said soberly. "Truth is, I. . .don't want you to go. I'm asking you not to take that other job."

"B–but. . .but I. . ." Myriad emotions played across her fragile features.

Lucas hadn't had an inkling that someone so vocal as Annora could ever be rendered speechless, yet apparently that was precisely the case. Having that first ever glimpse into the depth of her vulnerability, he knew how easily he could take advantage of her, if that was what he wanted.

It wasn't.

He did want her to come back. . .but only by her own

choice. And the only way to accomplish that entailed being completely honest, baring his soul. Time would permit nothing less. He shored up his insides and filled his lungs. "What would you think of staying on at the hotel for awhile?"

"I don't understand," Annora said softly. "Why would I do that?"

"Because, it would give me a chance to court you."

She paled, and her slender brows rose high. "Y–you want to court me?"

He nodded. "I've been a rotten employer, I know—or at least, I was in the beginning. I figured a whole raft of prospects would apply for the job, giving me a chance to pick and choose the one most suitable. I never believed someone like you could possibly do—*be*—all that I needed. But you proved me wrong. You were *and are* far beyond what I ever could've expected."

As Annora's emerald eyes softened, he pressed on. "The girls absolutely adore you. And I. . ." He feasted his gaze on her delicate beauty, the inner strength of character that gave wisdom beyond her years, and his whole being ached with tenderness. "I always surmised I would marry eventually, out of duty, so the girls would have a whole family again. What I didn't expect was to ever love again in my lifetime. . .that is, until you came along. I'm in love with you, Annora Nolan."

Those beautiful eyes misted over. "I. . . Th–that's really—" She blinked away the moisture. "Do you mean that?"

"Do I mean it?" he asked huskily. With a soft moan, he smiled and drew her into his arms, not even trying to suppress the surging of his pulse throbbing against his ribs. . . against hers. "How could I not love you, my sweet Annora? You brought me back to life again. You made the house a home. You made my daughters laugh. You even made me look up again and see God. I want you to come back and be part of my life. Now. Always."

Annora could not believe this was happening. Never in her

wildest dreams had she imagined Lucas Brent would think of her as a woman. . .a desirable one. She only knew that he was dearer to her than her own life. He was all she ever wanted, more than she could hope for.

"I won't rush you," he said gently. "I'm willing to give you whatever time you need to decide whether or not this is something you want, too. And, to set your mind at ease, Noah realized he'd acted like a jerk, and he assures me he'll never treat you disrespectfully again."

So many, many incredible notions were playing havoc within Annora as she stood gazing into Lucas's soul. She focused on those well-formed lips that so often—and even still—had her wondering. . . Surprising even herself, she raised to tiptoe and ever so softly pressed her untried lips to his.

Annora felt him smile as he tightened his embrace and answered her tentative invitation in a kiss of utmost reverence.

She had expected to feel a bit apprehensive in his arms, even nervous. But instead she knew only peace, as if God Himself smiled down at the fulfillment of His glorious plan.

"Is that a yes?" he whispered against her hair.

A phrase he had once used popped into her mind as she smiled up at him. " 'If the prospect pleases. . .' "

A chuckle rumbled from deep inside as he hugged her breathless.

"I happen to love you, too, Lucas," she somehow finished. "And I would be honored to become your wife."

Love, deep and abiding, glowed from Lucas's eyes as he gazed down at Annora and slowly lowered his head, covering her lips with his in a kiss filled with unspoken promises.

When it ended an eternal moment later, he smiled. "I know two little angels who are going to love hearing our news. You have just made three people very happy."

"You mean, four," Annora whispered and slid her fingers into his big, strong hand.

epilogue

two years later

The breath of early autumn wafted across the porch, stirring tendrils of Annora's hair about her face. She tucked the loose wisps behind her ear and adjusted the blanket surrounding her two-month-old son, Matthew Lucas. Soon the days would turn too cool for the luxury of sitting outside for the mere pleasure of it.

"May I please hold him, Mama?" Melinda asked as she bounded up the steps, sun streaks glistening in her dark, shiny hair.

Annora smiled lovingly at her stepdaughter. The girl had sprouted like a weed during the long hot summer, and now at eight years of age, she seemed happiest when mothering her new baby brother or helping about the house.

"Sure, sweetheart." Annora stood while Melinda took possession of the padded rocking chair and positioned herself comfortably. "Remember to hold his head," she coached gently and placed the chubby infant in his sister's arms.

"I will. Oh, look," she breathed, a dreamy smile widening her cheeks, "he's starting to get some hair again!"

"Yes, I noticed."

Chuckling to herself over how Matthew's tiny face had seemed so much rounder after losing the thick black hair of birth, Annora lightly stroked the velvety copper growth, a shade lighter than her own. His eyes, however, were the same dusky blue as his father's. "I'm going to go and see what Amy's up to. I'll be back in a few minutes."

Already absorbed in admiring the baby, Melinda only nodded.

But even as Annora stepped onto the front path, the sound of an approaching buggy carried from the lane. Pausing, she raised a hand to shield her eyes, trying to make out the two occupants of the conveyance.

Suddenly her heart leapt. Could it be?

"Lesley!"

Disregarding the propriety of her station as an old married lady and mother, Annora grasped her skirts in both hands and ran to meet the carriage.

"Surprise, surprise," her best friend said gleefully as her new husband, Michael Porter, drew up on the reins, halting the splendid dapple gray horse. Lesley clambered down every bit as unceremoniously as Annora and grabbed her in a huge hug.

"I can't believe this is real!" Annora gasped, trying to catch her breath. "And just look at you!" Easing the slender young woman to arm's length, she assessed Lesley's fashionable traveling suit and satin-trimmed bonnet, both in a rich sapphire blue that deepened the shade of her eyes and complemented her abundant honey-blond curls. Had it been anyone else, Annora would have felt conscious of her own everyday attire, but her incredible joy pushed such inconsequential thoughts aside.

"Hey, am I ever gonna get a hug?" Michael's deep voice teased as he tapped Annora on the shoulder.

She turned, and meeting the sparkle in those chocolate brown eyes, she flung her arms around his tall, muscular frame. He was clad equally elegantly in a dove gray pinstripe suit and bowler. "Oh, it's so wonderful that you've come here like this! You never mentioned a word of it."

"We wanted to surprise you," Lesley replied. "Michael's parents insisted on giving us a honeymoon trip to remember. . . so we immediately chose Wyoming. That way, we could not only take in the wonders of Yellowstone but visit you, as well." She turned a delicate rose. "Of course, I realize our dropping in on you might very well be an imposition. . .in which case—"

"Oh, I'll not hear a word of that," Annora said emphatically. "Of course you're welcome to stay with us for as long as you like. Come on, both of you, and I'll give you the grand tour, introduce you to my family—all but Noah, that is. He moved on to new adventures several months ago."

"Yes, do," Lesley agreed. "I'm dying to meet Lucas and the girls—to say nothing of your first little one."

Still smiling, Annora linked arms with Lesley and began strolling toward the recently painted house with its added rooms and neatly trimmed shrubbery, while Michael climbed back into the buggy and followed behind them.

"So, your wedding went smoothly?" Annora wanted to know. "Oh, I so would have loved to have been there, but with a new baby. . ."

"Yes, it was fine—except for the weather and the cake," Lesley said. "It poured so hard that day I wondered if anyone would bother to show up, but fortunately most Philadelphians aren't in the least put off by a little rain. A nice crowd attended—drooping hats and all. The cake, I'm afraid, didn't fare quite as well."

"Whatever happened?"

Lesley smothered a giggle. "When it was being carried to the church basement, a gust of wind caught the umbrella and tore it out of my mother's hands, leaving the icing to the mercy of the elements."

"It was rather pathetic," Michael piped in. "Especially after Mom and Dad Clark's hard work to make it special."

"I would imagine," Annora said. "But I'm sure it still tasted all right."

"Yes, that it did," Lesley said, nodding. "But what surprised me most, believe it or not, was how really sweet and helpful Mirah Thornby was throughout the entire occasion."

"You're not serious," Annora protested.

"Oh, but I am. It's amazing how a year and a half of marriage and an extremely difficult confinement can bring about some rather vast changes in a person. She was so thankful to deliver her healthy little daughter, she went through a transformation, finally confessing to her parents her horrid treatment of you. Mirah and the Baxters prevailed upon me to bring along their letters of apology. I have them in my valise."

Humbled and thankful for the answers to her prayers, Annora's spirit lightened considerably.

A look of wonder settled over her friend's fine features as they reached the porch and went up the steps. "Don't tell me that pretty little charmer is Melinda?"

"She sure is," Annora said proudly. "And a better, more loving helper a new mom could never find." Crossing to her, she laid a hand on the girl's shoulder. "Sweetheart, I'd like you to meet my very best friend in the whole world. This is Lesley Cl—I mean, Porter," she corrected, "and that's her husband, Michael, coming up the steps. Les, Michael, this is my daughter, Melinda. And this," she added, gently picking up the slumbering infant, "is Matthew Lucas." She placed him in Lesley's outstretched arms.

"Ohhh," Lesley crooned, caressing the tiny cheeks with her fingertips. "He is absolutely precious. You are so fortunate, Nora." She hugged him close, burying her nose in the soft bundle as she nestled him lovingly against her.

"I gather that must be the man of the house," Michael said, tipping his head in the direction of the barn.

Annora turned to see Lucas striding toward them, holding flaxen-haired Amy by the hand. Her heart nearly burst with pride at the sight of his manly bearing, the light of love in both his and their daughter's faces.

"Thought I heard someone drive up," Lucas said, removing his Stetson and raking a hand through his hair. He swept a glance over the gathering as he and Amy reached the porch.

"Lucas, I'm sure you've heard me talk often enough about

Lesley and Michael, my dear friends from Philadelphia."

"Ah. . .the ones who played such an important role in bringing our beautiful Annora into our lives. Finally I have the pleasure of meeting you. It is an honor." Flashing a warm grin, Lucas took Lesley's gloved hand and then Michael's.

"We feel the same, I assure you," Lesley said, blushing becomingly.

"Annora deserves whatever happiness the Lord brings her way," Michael offered.

"Oh, now, you two," Annora cajoled. Placing her hands on Amy's shoulders, she inched the little girl forward. "And this is Amy, our little horsewoman."

"You like horses?" Lesley asked, stooping to smile at the winsome beauty.

"Uh-huh. My pa bought me a pony. His name is Star."

"Well, you'll have to show me your pony soon, all right?"

She nodded. "Sissy has one, too, named Moonbeam. And Pa has lots of horses." She gestured toward the fenced pastureland occupied by an assortment of energetic colts and serene mares.

"I glimpsed a few as we came down the lane. I can't wait to see them all."

"Well, that will have to wait," Annora declared. "I'm sure you're both tired and thirsty. Let's go have some refreshments. The Lord has blessed us with this very special day, and we've got a lot of catching up to do."

Annora smiled up at Lucas, this wonderful man who had gifted a lonely girl with his love and his family, and she slipped into the crook of his arm. He gave her a squeeze, and together they led the happy group inside.

A Letter To Our Readers

Dear Reader:

In order that we might better contribute to your reading enjoyment, we would appreciate your taking a few minutes to respond to the following questions. We welcome your comments and read each form and letter we receive. When completed, please return to the following:

Rebecca Germany, Fiction Editor
Heartsong Presents
PO Box 719
Uhrichsville, Ohio 44683

1. Did you enjoy reading *If the Prospect Pleases?*
   ❏ Very much. I would like to see more books
      by this author!
   ❏ Moderately
      I would have enjoyed it more if _____

      _____

      _____

2. Are you a member of **Heartsong Presents**? Yes ❏ No ❏
   If no, where did you purchase this book?_____

   _____

3. How would you rate, on a scale from 1 (poor) to 5 (superior), the cover design?_____

4. On a scale from 1 (poor) to 10 (superior), please rate the following elements.

   _____ Heroine   _____ Plot

   _____ Hero   _____ Inspirational theme

   _____ Setting   _____ Secondary characters

5. These characters were special because_____

_____

_____

6. How has this book inspired your life?_____

_____

_____

7. What settings would you like to see covered in future
   Heartsong Presents books?_____

_____

_____

8. What are some inspirational themes you would like to see
   treated in future books?_____

_____

_____

9. Would you be interested in reading other **Heartsong
   Presents** titles?   Yes ❑   No ❑

10. Please check your age range:
    ❑ Under 18   ❑ 18-24   ❑ 25-34
    ❑ 35-45   ❑ 46-55   ❑ Over 55

11. How many hours per week do you read?_____

Name _____

Occupation _____

Address _____

City _____ State _____ Zip _____

......Heart♥ng ......

HEARTSONG PRESENTS TITLES AVAILABLE NOW:

(If ordering from this page, please remember to include it with the order form.)

·········· Presents ··········

Great Inspirational Romance at a Great Price!

Heartsong Presents books are inspirational romances in contemporary and historical settings, designed to give you an enjoyable, spirit-lifting reading experience. You can choose wonderfully written titles from some of today's best authors like Peggy Darty, Sally Laity, Tracie Peterson, Colleen L. Reece, Lauraine Snelling, and many others.

*When ordering quantities less than twelve, above titles are $2.95 each.
Not all titles may be available at time of order.*

Hearts♥ng Presents
Love Stories Are Rated G!

That's for godly, gratifying, and of course, great! If you love a thrilling love story, but don't appreciate the sordidness of some popular paperback romances, **Heartsong Presents** is for you. In fact, **Heartsong Presents** is the *only inspirational romance book club*, the only one featuring love stories where Christian faith is the primary ingredient in a marriage relationship.

Sign up today to receive your first set of four, never before published Christian romances. Send no money now; you will receive a bill with the first shipment. You may cancel at any time without obligation, and if you aren't completely satisfied with any selection, you may return the books for an immediate refund!

Imagine. . .four new romances every four weeks—two historical, two contemporary—with men and women like you who long to meet the one God has chosen as the love of their lives. . .all for the low price of $9.97 postpaid.

To join, simply complete the coupon below and mail to the address provided. **Heartsong Presents** romances are rated G for another reason: They'll arrive *Godspeed!*